THE ELEVEN QUESTIONS

EVERYTHING YOU EVER WANTED TO KNOW ABOUT LIFE, DEATH, AND AFTERLIFE

by Mark Pitstick

With exclusive contributions from Raymond Moody, Caroline Myss, Anita Moorjani, Gary Schwartz, Bernie Siegel, Stan Grof, Bill Guggenheim, P.M.H. Atwater, Marilyn Schlitz, Karen Wyatt, and Mark Anthony

All inquiries should be addressed to Mark R. Pitstick, MA, DC
mark@soulproof.com
www.soulproof.com
740-701-9793

The Eleven Questions: Everything You Ever Wanted To Know About Life, Death, and Afterlife
by Dr. Mark R. Pitstick

$14.95 US
ISBN-10 1-941768-91-1
ISBN-13 978-1-941768-91-4

Designed by:

R2 MEDIA GROUP PUBLICATIONS
A division of R2 Media Group
PO Box 4357 Pocatello, ID 83205
www.r2mg.com

DEDICATION

To my parents, Virginia and Bill Pitstick, who encouraged me to ask
questions and delighted in discussing the possibilities.

ACKNOWLEDGEMENTS

My gratitude to the esteemed guests who contributed exclusive material from
our radio shows together: Raymond Moody, PhD, MD; Caroline Myss, MA;
Anita Moorjani, Bernie Siegel, MD; Stan Grof, MD, PhD; Gary Schwartz, PhD;
Bill Guggenheim, P.M.H. Atwater, LHD.; Marilyn Schlitz, PhD;
Karen Wyatt, MD; Mark Anthony, JD.

To Andy for her love, support, and inspiration.

To my beloved daughters Faith and Rae Lynn

To Ryan Roghaar and Ana Martínez López for their
book design and setup wizardry

To Dr. Paul Brown and Lainey Ebright for final proofing.

To my agent Bill Gladstone and managing editor Kenneth Kales
for all their assistance.

To Spirit/Universe/Source for our daily walk together
through all of life's adventures.

IV THE ELEVEN QUESTIONS

TABLE OF CONTENTS

Introduction...............................1

Who am I?................................9

Why am I here?........................19

What happens after I die? 33

Is there a God/Source
Energy/ Higher Power?.............47

Why is there so
much suffering?........................57

Will I see my departed
loved ones again?.....................73

Are there ghosts
and evil spirits? 89

What happens to the soul/
life-force of people who
commit suicide? 101

How can I best hear my inner
self's voice and know my
highest purposes? 113

How can I evolve beyond past
religious teachings that don't
make sense to me now? 125

How can this information help me
better handle life's toughest
challenges and make the world a
better place? 137

Afterword..................................149

Guests' biographies...................151

Next steps..................................171

About the author 173

VI THE ELEVEN QUESTIONS

INTRODUCTION

While working in hospitals forty years ago, some patients touched me more than others.

Stevie was one such patient. A cute two-year-old boy with big brown eyes and a sad smile, he was a frequent visitor to the pediatric ward. First a broken leg, then a broken arm, then fractured ribs. His mother and her boyfriend shrugged and claimed he was just a very active toddler. I felt sorry for the little guy and visited when I could to try to cheer him up.

Then, one afternoon, I was the respiratory therapist assigned to the ER and was paged for a Code 4—a life-threatening emergency. I ran down there and was told the squad had called to say they were bringing in a little boy who was in severe condition. I met the ambulance team as they brought him into the treatment room. I took the boy from them and put him on the exam table. I felt a slight tugging as I removed my hands from his bare back and, in horror, saw that my hands were covered with dead skin from his body.

It was Stevie.

The doctors couldn't find a pulse or a good vein for an IV. His respirations were very shallow and he was severely dehydrated. There was nothing we could do and he died shortly after arriving to the ER. Soon, the back-story filtered in to the staff. The mother had been gone and the boyfriend was giving him a bath. The water was so hot that the little boy basically cooked to death. The police were charging him for negligent homicide. In hindsight, it appeared that his previous fractures were more than just being a very active child.

You know how life on earth can be.

Just watch or read the news any given day and you'll see the list: crime, murder, abuse, accidents, violence, war, starvation, rape, addiction.

Then look at your own life and review the litany of past and present pains and disappointments: illness, disability, divorce, lost relationships, broken dreams, injustices, financial loss, prejudice, cruelty, and so on.

You know the list.

Sometimes these events serve as "wake up calls" that shake up your world and make you ask important questions. At other times, they just further fracture your desire to be on this planet. You might have stared at the ceiling at night trying to make sense of your life and world events. You may have looked up at clear night skies, saw the vastness of creation and wondered, "What in the world is going on? Who am I? Why am I here? What happens when I die?"

You know the questions.

I've seen much suffering and pain and have been with many people as they died. I've read and watched the horrific news stories of how humans treat each other and themselves. I've looked at the ceiling and the stars and asked those questions.

Over the last four decades, I've searched long and hard to come up with sensible answers to life's toughest questions. I want to share my answers—and those of other esteemed searchers—with you

THE PAST

In the past, humans tried to make sense of suffering and death in a number of ways. Some attempted to control others and their environment by being the strongest and most powerful in the tribe. Others developed superstitions and rituals in an attempt to placate angry gods, forces of nature, or fate. More philosophical individuals developed personal cosmologies as they tried to understand the ways of the world.

Some people used consciousness-altering drugs and drinks in an attempt to discover meaningful answers to life's greatest quandaries. For some, these methods birthed powerful spiritual insights. For others, they led to overuse, disorientation, and addiction.

Still others developed a passive acceptance of life. They sunk into disempowered beliefs that life on earth is meant for suffering, that it has always been that way and always will be.

Consciously or unconsciously, all of them probably wondered about the most puzzling *existential* questions: "Why do we exist? What is this existence all about?"

Over time, spiritual/religious teachers surfaced in different times and cultures. Usually, they helped those in surrounding villages, but sometimes they gained widespread popularity. Their lessons were designed to teach people with varying degrees of intelligence and understanding so they taught with parables, myths and stories.

Over time, sects or denominations formed around these more popular teachers. Some of these acknowledged that their teachings were metaphorical and best understood through great stories. Others, particularly those with more zealous or fundamental views, maintained that their teachings were to be taken literally and were the only true way to God and salvation.

In the Middle Ages, very few people could read and books were scarce. Ever-more-powerful clergy handed down "the gospel truth"—sometimes in a foreign language—to trusting congregants. Councils of powerful men voted on what teachings to include or discard from holy books. Well-meaning scribes added references to contemporary events so their scriptures were more relevant.

Books written by several different authors over time were misrepresented as being written by one disciple who personally knew the original teacher. Eventually, the errors, omissions, additions, mistranslations, and interpretations accumulated to significant proportions. Some current day scholars question how much of the original teachings actually survived.

The original teachers may have believed that their words were inspired by God, or that claim may have been added afterwards. In either case, religious teachings were clearly changed by humans. It's a historical fact.

At times, political rulers adopted fledgling religious sects to strengthen their kingdoms and consolidate beliefs of their minions. Powerful clergy joined forces with ambitious rulers in a bizarre marriage of church and state. Abuses of trust were rampant as those in control predictably succumbed to the temptations of money and power.

Paradoxically, many religious teachings from before and during the Medieval Ages are still in vogue. In no other discipline—health care, transportation, technology, etc.—do we rely on millennia old understandings. But many people still do with religious teachings that are patently nonsensical.

It's been a mess. We in the 21st century can do better than that.

THE 21ST CENTURY

Fortunately, we currently live in an unprecedented time in the history of humanity. The Internet, social media, and other rapid information dispersal technologies allow nearly instantaneous sharing of information among individuals—not just from mainstream media sources.

More people are increasingly difficult to control and deceive. They are thinking for themselves and no longer accepting the status quo. They can read and vast information resources are available. They want to know sensible, evidence-based answers to life's most important questions.

They and you are in luck. A vast and varied amount of clinical, scientific, religious/spiritual, and empirical (based on firsthand experience) evidence now exists. Optimal answers and solutions to our greatest problems can be found by merging wise spirituality teachings, contemporary findings, and your inner knowing.

These answers are very important as they form the very framework that allows you to live and die with peace, joy, clarity, and purpose. Wise answers help you survive and even thrive throughout life's toughest challenges.

The Eleven Questions shares my answers and those of some of the most renowned experts on consciousness topics. I gave them the most commonly asked questions about life, death, and afterlife that I've received from people all around the world. Their answers from our radio interviews have been lightly edited for printed versus audio use.

THE QUESTIONS

1. Who am I?

2. Why am I here? If I really am an infinite being of energy/consciousness/spirit, why in the world would I want to visit a place like Earth?

3. What happens after I die? If there's an afterlife, is it the same for everyone or are there different possible experiences?

4. Is there a God/Higher Power/Source? If there is, what is this phenomenon like and what is our relationship to It?

5. Why is there suffering? This issue is especially difficult to understand when children suffer and die.

6. Will I see my departed loved ones again? If so, how can I best communicate with them now?

7. Are there really ghosts and evil spirits? What are they?

8. What happens to the soul/life-force of people who commit suicide?

9. How can I best hear my inner self's voice and know my highest purposes?

10. How can I evolve beyond my earlier religious teachings that don't make sense to me now? Examples are teachings about an eternal hell, we were born into sin, there's only one true religion, being gay is sinful, etc.

11. How can this information help me deal with my toughest challenges and make the world a better place?

A FINAL WORD

Some of my answers are evidence-based, that is, they stem from documented clinical and scientific research. Other answers arise from empirical evidence, that is, from my personal and professional firsthand experiences. Finally, my beliefs—shaped by the factors above, my training, and more—figure into my answers to these questions.

It's the same with the eleven top experts in consciousness studies who shared their answers to life's biggest questions. I wanted to share their insights because of their impressive backgrounds, experiences, hearts, and minds.

We don't claim to have all the answers, or the only answers, but we do have some very good answers that have helped many people make more sense of this earth-experience.

You'll notice that some guests' answers are quite different. This isn't reason for concern or discounting the information in general. We each are like blind people discovering an elephant for the first time. Our descriptions will understandably vary given our different backgrounds. After reading our viewpoints, consider what makes the most sense to you. A more informed world-view can only result in enhanced growth, compassion, and harmony.

1 WHO AM I?

ANITA MOORJANI

I want people to know that who you are is much more and much greater than this physical body. Most of us are conditioned to see that all we are is this physical body and we are limited to what our physical body can do and be. Most of our upbringing and education is focused very much on physical reality. We're so focused on what we can see, hear, and feel but in actuality there's a whole other dimension that is not brought to our attention. In many cases, we are laughed at or pooh-poohed if we do have experiences where we touch this other reality.

In actuality, we are so much more than this physical body. I'm going to call it consciousness, but we can call it spirit, soul, it doesn't really matter. We can even call it God. Who we really are is *pure consciousness* and it is much bigger than our bodies, more powerful. When I sense myself as consciousness, I realize that my soul is connected to yours and it's connected to everyone else.

There's no separation. Our bodies may lead us to believe that we are separate, but when we actually get in touch with who we really are, we realize that we're all connected. We're all expressions of the same consciousness, but we're different expressions. When I became aware of who I really am, I realized that is the truth. When I knew—with every cell of my body—that I am so much greater, I am one with everything, I am one with God—I realized that my body was just a reflection of my realization of that state. As soon as I realized that, my body healed. I want people to know that they are much more powerful, amazing and magnificent than they have been led to believe.

P.M.H. ATWATER

I truly am an immortal soul, an extension of the Divine who temporarily resides within a carbon-based form of electromagnetic pulsations that produces a solid-appearing overlay of behavior patterns more commonly referred to as a personality. So I'm a soul. Who I really am is not my personality. My personality and the body I'm wearing enables me to carry out the plan, but who I am is part of what I call the one God.

MARK PITSTICK

Humans can only sense a tiny fraction of life. Many quantum physicists agree that the average person perceives less than one percent of reality. They say that the most absolute understanding is that "solid matter" is comprised of light and energy. Further, they say that if all the light and energy in our world were the size of Mt. Everest, the portion we can usually perceive with our five senses would be the size of a golf ball.

So, it's as though you've been looking through a little pinhole in a wall trying to understand what's going on. One important question to ask yourself is, "How can I open that pinhole a bit and make more sense of life?"

You are a timeless being of energy, spirit, consciousness, and awareness. A soul. You are a being of light who is temporarily living in a human form so you can function in this physical world. You are an integral and infinite part of All That Is. God can be likened to a divine ocean and you are like a drop of water in that ocean, but a very important drop. If it weren't for all those drops of water, the ocean would be diminished.

Water can be in the form of steam, liquid, or ice, but—no matter what the outward appearance—it's all water. Similarly, your outward appearance may change, but your essence persists. You may or may not have a body depending on what time and place you're living in, but your energy/real self exists throughout and beyond those changes. Lots of evidence clearly indicates that your consciousness survives physical death and existed before birth. You are what I call a WISP, an acronym for a "Wise, Infinite, Special and Powerful" being.

By the way, when people hear about humans as eternal beings of consciousness/energy/ awareness, they sometimes ask, "What about the part of me that likes being in nature, my loved ones, great food, cliffhanger movies and books, and so on? What happens to all that if I'm just a being of energy?"

The good news is that everything you've ever done and been becomes part of who you are. You don't lose anything as you journey through forever—you are much more than you could ever realize. Your personality, memories, preferences and skills all become part of your totality.

Over time, your lower and more negative aspects burn away. Your essence/energy becomes higher and more refined. You awaken to the high being of light and love that you always were and live accordingly.

MARILYN SCHLITZ

I think we are always answering that question in different ways depending on our life circumstances and stages in our personal growth. There's obviously the "I" that operates in life, has relationships, goes to a job, gets educated, etc. And then there is an opportunity to shift toward what people describe as the larger "I," the "we," that is transcendent of our physical being and that we can connect to through spiritual practices. Even quantum physics now sheds light for us on what it means to be interconnected.

After years of research looking at transformations in consciousness, we've seen that at the core can be what we call a *noetic impulse*. That is some kind of direct personal experience in which people use the first person pronoun "I" as in, "I had a near-death experience." "I had an out-of-body experience." "I had some kind of mystical" experience." These experiences can be triggered in very simple ways: in one case a person was washing dishes, looked out the window, and shifted her perspective of who and what the "I" meant to her. These are ways in which the direct experience of "I" becomes fundamental in the growth toward a larger sense of "we."

It can be more difficult for some people who resist these new impulses. Sometimes our brains are very capable of not learning new things.

GARY SCHWARTZ

I'm going to speak as a scientist, not from my own personal experience. Yes, we each are clearly more than just a human body. From everything we know in contemporary physics, everything that exists is a combination of what we call energy and information. What we mean by matter, what we experience as matter, is actually organized energy. And the interesting thing about information and energy is that, in the vacuum of space, it's there forever.

So for example, if we look at the sky at night and we're out in the country away from city lights there's no moon, there's no clouds, we see the light of thousands of stars. With telescopes, we can see billions of galaxies, each with billions of stars. All that light has been traveling for millions and billions of years in the vacuum of space and it doesn't disappear. If it became "randomized," if it became distorted in the vacuum of space, then you and I would look at the sky at night and see mush. But we don't see mush, we see a history of star light going back millions and billions of years.

Light has a kind of "immortality" and the energy/information of humans is like distant stars. And that includes, by the way, what we call our thoughts, our feelings, our personalities, our consciousness. Just a basic understanding of physics, particularly quantum physics, leads us to the conclusion that our essence is like the essence of matter itself. It's information and energy which sounds very much like soul and spirit.

CAROLINE MYSS

That's a question that many people ask, but usually later in life. It's a question one asks in layers. Somewhere in the middle years of our lives perhaps we ask that from a deeper level. It becomes a question that redirects how we want to experience life: from seeing life as something we take from to seeing life as something we give to. So the question "Who am I?" becomes a discovery of the potential we have to change the quality of the lives of others versus just our own lives.

There are individuals who come to that question because their lives are falling apart, they've read a lot of spiritual literature, they're naturally philosophically inclined, or they've been ill and brought to death's door. So there are different routes that lead people to that question.

Human nature is such that we are inherently designed to seek out the sacred even if that's not the language a person uses for it. Human beings gravitate toward experiences of the sacred in layers. People want to feel important, they have a disdain for the ordinary. That's their first motivation to seek the extraordinary and after the extraordinary comes the sacred. And so at some point along that trajectory, a person will ask "Who am I?"

BILL GUGGENHEIM

My background was and still is Christian so my answer may be partially influenced by that. When I was young, I was taught that when we die some part of us called our soul leaves our body. If we were good little boys and girls, the soul goes *up* to something called heaven; and if we were bad, it goes *down* to a place called hell. That didn't feel right to me. That didn't seem to jell.

What I believe now is that each of us—you, I, everyone—is a spirit or soul or being of light right here, right now. We each are wearing a physical body, *an earth suit* that we need to do all the different things that human beings do. Our earth suits can take a great deal of use and abuse over time, but at some point they cease to work.

I liken it very much to a space suit that astronauts wear. If an astronaut goes outside the spacecraft and the space suit is punctured, it ceases to operate and the wearer will die. The same is true for a deep sea diver who wears a large metal helmet and pressurized suits that can go to great depths. If that suit becomes damaged, the person wearing it will die. Same thing for your physical body. It has certain limits and will eventually cease to function.

BUT THE I THAT I AM AND THE YOU THAT YOU ARE IS IMMORTAL. We already have a spiritual body that very strongly resembles our physical body. We continue our existence in our spiritual body to the afterlife or life after death that has many names. In our book, we often referred to the afterlife as heaven, but it could be called nirvana, paradise, or any other name you care to give it. Different religions have different names for this place.

BERNIE SIEGEL

That's easy. My way of is saying it is when you get to heaven and you are in the admission line and they say "You're next, how do you want to be introduced to God?" If you say I'm a doctor, God says "Come back when you know who you are." So who I'm I? I'm God's child or God. Either one gets you in. So, how do I identify myself? I'm one of God's family, one of God's children.

STAN GROF

Before I answer the questions, I would like to say I am not a guru so I'm not saying, "This is the way it is." I have researched *non-ordinary states of consciousness* for over half a century, and in particular, a subgroup of these states that I believe have healing, transformative, and evolutionary potential. They also have *heuristic potential* which means you can learn new information about consciousness, the psyche, even about the nature of reality. My answers are based on what I have seen or heard from people who had these experiences—my clients, people in our training and workshops—and also experiences that I've had in these states myself.

I was very surprised that psychiatry does not have a name for this important subgroup of states that shamans, initiates, and yogis experience. So I gave them a name "holotropic" from root words for "whole" and "moving." I'm talking about states that take us in the direction of wholeness. Some people say, "Well, aren't we whole already in the way we experience ourselves in everyday life?" I say, "No, because in these non-ordinary states, we can expand our consciousness and experience various aspects of the universe as our personal experience."

Ultimately, the term holotropic suggests something that the Hindus and many other traditions described, that our true identity is a spark of divine energy that we carry in our innermost being. Hindus call it *Atman* and they have practices that allow you to actually experience it. This clearly validates who you ultimately are. When you have the experience of *Atman*, you realize that your energy is identical with the creative energy of the universe that is called *Brahman*. So your true identity is with Atman-Brahman, not with the body-ego as we call it.

KAREN WYATT

We are souls who came to this planet to experience a physical lifetime. Our souls are who we really are. This earthly identity is just our temporary facade while we're here on Earth.

Our souls have probably been here for many lifetimes in the past. Even as children, many people have a high level of spiritual awareness and knowledge. As souls, we have opportunities to evolve. Some of the knowledge and wisdom we have was actually brought with us to this incarnation.

We are unique manifestations of the Infinite Creative Source and are made up of the same stardust as the Universe. And yet, we are totally distinct in our physical forms into which we have incarnated. We are spirits who have incarnated in the material realm in order to manifest every possible aspect of creativity and love. We have unique soul identities that guide our lives on this planet and that will persist after our physical forms fade away.

MARK ANTHONY

Human beings are actually multi-dimensional beings. We're infinite and immortal spirits that are temporally tethered to a body. One of the best ways to explain this is to think of a wine bottle with a cork in it. Our souls are currently encapsulated in bodies like a bottle and our brains are like a cork. Our brains are judges about reality but can only sense the finite world, everything that you and I know and can experience.

However, the other side, the afterlife, is infinite. There are reasons that we are here to experience a finite, limited existence. When it's time to leave the material world, the brain—which houses fear, ego and limitation—is released like a cork and our spirits revert back to their immortal states.

But there's more to it than that because we also have an eternal component. On one level, we experience a material world existence; at the same time, however, our higher selves are still connected to God, to the collective consciousness, to the other side. *(Mark Anthony, the Psychic Lawyer, author of Never Letting Go and Evidence of Eternity)*

RAYMOND MOODY

You know the greatest people have struggled with this one. What is that essence, that centerpiece of yourself that makes you the unique person you are? I was kind of a philosophically-inclined kid. I remember having this conversation with myself as a young child: "This consciousness thing is pretty weird. I mean, how this can be?" My first passion was astronomy and that really wakes you up. You see the vastness out there and that focuses your attention on being conscious now. From the very beginning, I've suspected that the consciousness is in charge. Where I am with it now is probably quite startling: I think the self is a narrative self.

Elie Wiesel survived Auschwitz and after the war became a Nazi hunter. He was a very wise man who said, "God made man because He loves stories." If you think about it, what is a human life but a story? During my work as a geriatric psychiatrist, I spoke with lots of older people who were depressed or having situational stress or grief. These very articulate people said, "At some point, you develop an uncanny impression that your life has been a sort of a play." I heard Joseph Campbell, the mythologist say that too. And now, at the age of 69, I am beginning to sense this myself.

As we go along through life, we weave our life's stories, we tell our life stories. Plato looked at this and said there is an immaterial entity that inhabits the physical substance of the body. He called it a soul entity. That is a word that is very important to all of us. At the same time, that idea is very difficult to put into words. Exactly what is it? There have been fights about it all through the centuries.

In the 17th century, John Locke—in the wake of the collapse of the church's authority— said that what he thought constituted the self-identity was your memories. Then Hume came along and said, as he looks inside of himself, he sees ideas, sensations and perceptions that are just flowing. So, that's the status of the philosophical debate but, as for me, I've come around to a narrative concept of it.

2 WHY AM I HERE?

IF I AM AN INFINITE BEING OF ENERGY AND PART OF GOD,
WHY IN THE WORLD WOULD I COME TO A PLACE LIKE EARTH?

ANITA MOORJANI

Believe it or not, we choose it. I know many people might say, "Why would I choose to come to earth when I could be in much more amazing states?" We choose it for the experience. I like to kid around and say, "I came here for the chocolate because there's no chocolate in the other realm." In this realm we have a physical body and we get to experience certain things like tasting food and making passionate love. Physical feelings can be experienced here in a physical body that we can't experience in that nonphysical dimensions.

In spiritual realms, what we feel is amazing and expansive and we feel unconditional love all the time. On earth, we get to actually experience and figure out who we truly are. We get to experience challenges and realize that heaven is a state of consciousness, not a place. I wanted to come here to experience that. As long as we know who we truly are, it doesn't really matter whether we're here or whether we're there. We can experience heaven right here with a physical body.

P.M.H. ATWATER

Why would I want to visit earth? We are all here with jobs to do and missions to perform. We are here to remember who we are.

We enter this world on an in-breath and we leave this world on an out-breath. Life is composed of back and forth, motion and rest. It's part of our coming and going. Whether it's tragic or happy—it doesn't matter. Some of us stay on earth for a few hours, a few months, a few years, many decades, but all of it is important. Every breath is important. We're all part of that greater matrix, that greater expression.

The curriculum is "over there", the other side, heaven, however you want to define that. But we develop our muscles over here, on earth. This is where we take that spiritual curriculum and act it out. Either we learn or we mess up, but we're still forming those muscles. That's what the earth life is all about. It's where we choose, experience, get mad, love, have joy, heal, help and grow. That's part of why we're here.

MARK PITSTICK

I use an acronym to help you remember why you're here: *sage*:

- *'S' stands for service:* helping others and following the Golden Rule. And, of course, whatever you give to others, you get back many times more.

- **'A' is for adventure:** that's one reason you probably like plays, books, and movies with heroes and heroines… because that's who you really are. It takes a brave soul to come to a place like Earth and have an exciting adventure. When you remember that, you are better able to handle the challenges. Whenever you play a game, it helps to know the rules. Well, two of the rules for being on earth are you volunteered for this experience and you helped co-create it. Recalling that helps you remember that, as Helen Keller said, life is either an amazing adventure or it is nothing at all.

- **'G' stands for growth:** Earth is one of the most sought after places for souls to incarnate because it's such a fruitful place for growth and learning. If you went to the gym and curled a pencil as your weight, you wouldn't get much bicep growth, would you? But if you curled a heavy dumbbell, you would get more muscle growth. Likewise, if life is easy all the time and everything is perfect, there's not the contrast, the resistance that helps you grow.

- **'E' stands for enjoyment.** Earth is a very beautiful place when you open your eyes and look at the positives as well as the negatives. There are certain enjoyments here that aren't available in the same way in non-physical realms. The movie Awakenings, based upon the book by Oliver Sacks, MD, tells the true story of patients who were in lethargic trances, a sort of sleeping sickness, for decades. A medical drug L-Dopa temporarily awakened them so they could enjoy the many splendors of life on earth. The movie beautifully depicted just how amazing life really is when you open your eyes and appreciate the beauty around you.

So, loving service, adventure, growth, and enjoyment are common reasons you, as a soul, would choose to visit a place like Earth.

Another reason your soul might come to Earth is to assist Life Itself in evolving. You are part of Source Energy right now. God is not a concrete or static entity, It's an expanding phenomenon. The cosmos is still learning and growing. I envision a vast amoeba-like phenomenon of love/energy/intelligence/light with many little extensions that experience new information and report back to the One. You are like one of those little pseudopods. While on Earth, you are experimenting and discovering. All that input gets reported back to the one Presence. It's a beautiful system and really mind blowing if you think about it for a while. But let me reassure you that your earth-experience is a totally safe and magnificent adventure through eternity.

MARILYN SCHLITZ

We are hard-wired to create stories about our lives and give meaning and purpose to them. Ultimately, having meaning—a sense of why we are here—is really important for everything: our happiness, physical well-being, relationship to our families and communities, and a sense of spirituality or religion. Some people spend a lot of time trying to answer the questions, "Am I here for some purpose and what is it?" They may answer these questions differently at different points in their life. Spiritual or transformational practices can help us get better answers to that question.

Often times, we are motivated to ask these questions when we have some kind of complex experience, some disruption in our lives. When everything's going along fine (or fine enough) we don't worry too much about, "Who I am and why am I here?" We're just busy living. And then something happens: the death of a loved one, loss of a job, divorce, something that destabilizes our steady state. And that can cause us to refocus and redefine what is our purpose. In that process, we have opportunities to increase the quality and authenticity of our relationships and self-care practices.

We can also redefine our relationship to broader meanings of the universe via spiritual, religious, or other approaches. These systems provide us with a great deal of meaning, important pathways into answering "Why am I here?" Ultimately, each of us has to answer that question for ourselves.

GARY SCHWARTZ

First of all, that's a great question. Why is a bird on the earth and why is an elephant on the earth? Why are any living systems on the earth? You could argue that we're here to learn life's lessons. We're here to grow. We're here to develop our "individual souls" and at some level, that's true. You could also say the same thing about lobsters, fish, tigers, and so on. All creatures are here to live out their respective lives.

But I think human beings have a bigger purpose than just that. We have the capacity to reflect on all of this and to be of service. My working hypothesis is that we're here not just to learn and grow, we're also here to develop the capacity to love, to increasingly appreciate, and take an ever-greater responsibility for things. It's not just to go back to heaven and be happier. We can be wiser parents and people who express love and caring now. That's my personal opinion as opposed to a scientific one.

I wrote a book called the *G.O.D. Experiments.* G.O.D. stands for guiding, organizing and designing process. At the end of this book, I have a chapter that says *infinite love is the ultimate gift from God.* A lesson occurred to me many years ago when I was a professor at Yale: human beings are like little love machines as we come onto the planet. We literally love everything and want to experience it. We're curious about everything. That only changes when we experience pain or our parents and teachers punish us for doing things. They teach we're not supposed to love this or we're not supposed to love that.

One of the things that's quite remarkable about the capacity for human love is illustrated in a university setting. There you have hundreds of professors from all walks of life pursuing their passions for questions whether they're about atoms in physics or molecules in chemistry. My father was a chemist and pharmacist who loved chemicals. People who are biologists spend their lives studying fruit flies or finches. Others fall in love with psychology, sociology, and on and on.

Human beings have the capacity to love almost any aspect of life and I think this is one of our defining qualities. And as people evolve in their "soul growth," they consider concepts such as universal love and unconditional love. We hear phrases such as "God loves everyone and everything" and that certainly was a message of great spiritual teachers like Jesus.

What I realized is that we're sort of "pre-programmed to love." We are designed with that capacity. That's what is so fascinating about the science, biology, and psychology of love. Love is a nearly untapped resource, but it requires education for us to manifest it. That's my greatest inspiration, to expand people's appreciation for their capacity to love and then to honor it.

CAROLINE MYSS

That's a question people ask because of their disdain for the ordinary. That's the beginning of their questions: I want to be important, I want some reason to be alive other than a shopping cart, other than an ordinary job. A job's not enough so I'll seek a career, but eventually a career is not enough. I want a vocation. I want a calling.

The majority of people I encounter exist between the frustration of having a job or career and the longing to have a calling. But they lack courage to go that distance, to actually bow their head, take their shoes off on sacred ground, and say "call me by name." They can't utter that prayer. They simply can't do it so they exist in a kind of spiritual no-man's land between this physical world and the inner world.

They can't go into the interior world for fear that it will swallow them up—their bank account, sensuality, sexuality, their whole physical world—and disorient them. So they go there only mentally, in conversation, in books, but they don't really go there experientially so they spend their life thinking "Why am I here?" And they go there with their ego: "I know I'm here to do something important." So they reduce it to career and glamour and the need to feel significant. They never get to the point of surrendering to living in that high voltage realm of *let my soul take over*.

Are our callings preset before this lifetime or how do they come about? We can only speculate about these matters. I base my perceptions on *the nature of nature* because we are creatures of nature so we're all subject to the same laws of nature. So you look at the way nature operates and you say, "Is the way the forest grows preset?" No, but it has an inclination, a proclivity to it, and it's the same with us.

Your being, intellect, archetypal structure has patterns to it that you're going to operate within. You are as expansive as those patterns, but they do contain you. You have endless choices within that, but what you do with it is up to you. How much effort and creativity you put into something is up to you. All of these things are in your hands; you're the engine of your destiny.

BILL GUGGENHEIM

We're here to learn how to love everyone unconditionally, including ourselves. It's all about love, acts of compassion, kindness, empathy, and the highest attributes. Life on earth is like a school and we are like students. We choose in advance what classes we'll take and what our various assignments will be and we go through them. We even choose our parents, grandparents, siblings, friends, enemies, spouse or spouses if we have more than one. We choose the circumstances—economic, political, and social—we enter into. We set up details of our school and the lessons that we'll learn from it.

Life on earth is very much like Disney World. It's like a theme park where we come to learn and act out various roles that we want to experience. Some people want to be a warrior; they enjoy it and when one war ends, they sign up to be a mercenary in another war. That fulfills them in some way. Other people want to be something totally different. Some people want to be a sheriff and arrest the bad guys while others want to be a bank robber.

Everything has a duality; there are two sides. People choose what we call good roles, but also in some cases choose the bad guy roles. Life on earth is like a play and we are like actors in a theater company that puts on a different play every week. We portray different characters in a comedy, drama, mystery, or action-filled play. That's what a lifetime on earth is. The key element is that we have multiple lifetimes and multiple learning opportunities. The books *Journey of Souls* and *Destiny of Souls* by Dr. Michael Newton do a good job of explaining why we souls come to earth.

BERNIE SIEGEL

The best answer I've heard was at a support group. I asked people, "Why are you here?" and one guy said," I'm here because I'm not all there."

I'm on the board of directors of heaven as a consultant and God is always talking in parables that confuse me. One day, God said, "You are a satellite dish, a remote control, and a television screen." And I said, "I don't understand what you are talking about." The answer was that there are many channels out there that you are like a satellite dish that can receive many different voices

---

speaking. Your mind is like a remote control, you can select what you listen to. And your body is like a television screen; it demonstrates what channels you are listening to.

The problem is, who is your God? What channels are you tuned into? When you see what the world is like, you know that a lot of people are tuned into the wrong channels: the material things, war and fighting, I'm right and you're wrong.

I'm here to be a love warrior, I use love as my weapon. If people drive me crazy, I love them. That confuses them, they don't know what to do with me. I know they are acting that way because they didn't grow up with love. What we are all here to do is to love each other so everyone knows they are worthwhile. The opposite of love is indifference, rejection and abuse. When you grow up with that, you are here for the wrong reasons. That can cause you to become self-destructive as well as destructive of others.

All you need to do is listen to the news, all the killing, violence, and suicides. It just goes on and on. Imagine walking into a school, not with a gun, but getting up on the stage in the auditorium and yelling out, "I love you, I love you, I love you." I've done that at high schools. A thousand kids were sitting there and I said, "I want you to know I love you and if you need a father, I'll be your father." One young lady who was suicidal told me I was "her CD—her chosen dad" and it helped her to know she was accepted by me.

I don't have to like how others are behaving, but I can love them. Then they come to love themselves, change their behavior, and become life-enhancing instead of self-destructive. We are here to live and learn.

STAN GROF

We went through records of about five thousand people from psychedelic sessions. We also had sessions with thousands of people using holotropic breathwork. They achieved nonordinary states of consciousness by breathing, powerful music, and certain kinds of bodywork. I summed up their answers, and these were certainly confirmed by my own experiences, in my book *The Cosmic Game*. People answered the questions: "Who am I? Where do I come from? Where am I going? What is this all about? Is this just a material universe that created itself or does it have a master blueprint? Does it have a creator?"

One person after another, particularly those who had these experiences repeatedly, identified the principles of the Atman and identified the cosmic creative energy. They saw this source of creation and asked, "What is my relationship to this principle and why does creation happen?" Ultimately, their answers were very similar to what you find in the spiritual scriptures of Hinduism, Buddhism, Kabbalah and so on.

This is an adventure in consciousness, experiencing the creative principle. The Divine wants to experience Itself. In Kabbalah, they say faith wanted to see faith. The Source has this incredible potential, but to get to know this potential, it has to be expressed. And it's expressed in creation, the world of polarity, the journey from oneness to plurality. It's expressed in the creation of these many fantastic universes, the realm of divine figures, demonic figures, the abodes of the beyond and so on to the material world as we experience it. So it's about *an adventure of self-discovery.*

KAREN WYATT

I believe the purpose for any lifetime is the soul's purpose to live through a physical lifetime in a physical body in order to learn lessons that the soul needs to acquire.

For example, the lessons I have been working on through this incarnation are learning how to synthesize power and humility. Those are themes that I have played out multiple times in my life. I'm learning how to manifest and utilize power while remaining humble at the same time. Another lesson I feel I'm here to learn is to synthesize freedom and responsibility... learning how to exercise freedom in life while remaining responsible for my actions and consequences of my behavior.

We each are here as unique souls incarnated in the physical realm in order to maximize the manifestation of love throughout the Universe and to acquire the knowledge necessary for growth. Life on this planet helps us learn how to transcend difficulties and attain our highest purposes: having unconditional love and manifesting Heaven on Earth. We are here to learn as much as we can from our life experiences.

MARK ANTHONY

That's one that people and religious and spiritual leaders have been asking themselves from the dawn of time. Based on what I can tell, it appears that we lead a series of material world incarnations. In the work I've done communicating with spirits, they all talk about going through several lifetimes.

In the field of near-death experience research, the majority of people talk about a belief in reincarnation. Reincarnation is at the root of all major religions—Hinduism, Buddhism, Judaism and Christianity. Ancient mystical sects of Judaism referred to a succession of lifetimes. Early Christian theologians such as Origin of Alexandria discussed leading a series of lives. He said that even Satan would eventually ascend into the Light.

The reason souls come to Earth is there are experiences and sensations that we cannot have while we're in an infinite state. The Other Side is without physical death, pain, illness, and old age. Here in the material world, we can experience things that we cannot over in the nonphysical. For whatever reasons, that appears to be important for our spiritual development in the long-term since the purpose of spirit is to continually evolve, grow and learn.

There's this notion in some traditional religions that, after you die, you stand before a throne and it's, "You were bad—DING—you go down to Hell." Or, "You were good—DING—you go up to Heaven." I'm not saying there aren't different levels on the Other Side, but that simplistic view of heaven or hell is based on medieval imagery. It's a male dominated version of the after life. When you start working with it, you see that it's a finite attempt by finite beings to put a face on the Infinite. *(Mark Anthony, the Psychic Lawyer, author of Never Letting Go and Evidence of Eternity)*

RAYMOND MOODY

I can take my thoughts about that from listening to thousands of people who had near-death experiences. They see the Light and then view their lives in this vivid panorama. They see everything they've ever done, it's right there in front of them instantaneously. People say they have to describe it as though it were in sequence because language is sequential. But they say that the experiencing of it is not sequential, that everything is there all at once. Very often, they say that they experience all this in the company of an illuminated being of Light. This being of complete compassion is there to help them review their lives. And they say that what stands out is, ***it's all about love and learning to love.***

In this panorama, they say, you see each action of your life but when you do, it's like looking at another person. You see yourself doing the actions and you are embedded in the consciousness of the person with whom you've interacted. If you see yourself doing something mean-spirited to that person, then you immediately feel the same feelings of sadness or pain. If you see yourself doing something loving, then you get the good feelings back. So, everyone comes back from this saying that it's all about love. We are here to learn from and experience everything.

You know, people in my profession and your profession might judge me as psychotic on what I am about to say, but I think here's the closest you can come to a description of what this earthly experience is about: we each are part of God's educational and entertainment media. There are seven billion of these little narrative threads weaving in and out and fitting in. Everyone's life is a little story that intercepts with someone else's for some period of time and then they diverge. If, as Wiesel said, God loves stories, just imagine the thrill He is getting out of this.

I recently read the most accurate account ever made of the number of stars in the known Universe: one hundred and fifty billion trillion. Now let's say that the average star has only four planets around it; that's six hundred billion trillion planets in just the known universe. Astronomers estimate that one out of one-thousand planets are earth-like and they've already detected some planets with the right type of sun and so on to support life. You've got to admit that this is an accomplishment.

Given all this, it's just amazing to me that while overseeing this vast creation, God is —as Pat Robertson and company think— concerned about two gay guys living together.

Why are we here? We live in an amazing universe and this is just an amazing existence we live.

3

WHAT HAPPENS AFTER I DIE?

WHAT ARE THE POSSIBILITIES?
IS THERE A SPECTRUM OF AFTERLIFE SCENARIOS?

ANITA MOORJANI

I'm going to offer my opinion that stems from my own experience of dying. I believe that after physical death, all of us go to a place of absolute unconditional love. There have been people who experienced hellish NDE's or lower levels. They may, for a short time, experience an afterlife *according to their beliefs at the time of passing*. It depends on how strong the mind is conditioned about hell and judgment and so on. But it's totally dependent on how strongly the mind holds on to those beliefs.

I believe that, at the point of death, we are still controlled by our minds for at least a little while, but eventually everyone moves on from that point. I very strongly believe that everyone eventually moves on to this place of absolute unconditional love. I absolutely do not believe in hell; that concept has been created by our conditioning.

Some people have hellish NDE's. I respect their experiences and am not dismissing them because I know they had real fear. But if they had stayed in that experience long enough, they would have come out of it and realized it was a result of conditioning. They would have realized we all can go to an amazing space where we feel extreme love and clarity about why we're here, what we want to do next, and so on. We will also meet up with our deceased loved ones and be able to watch over our loved ones who are still in physical bodies.

Time is very different in the afterlife than it is here in physical life. While on earth, we think in terms of what will we do next? But when we're not expressing in our physical body, time doesn't exist in a linear fashion. When I was in that NDE state, it felt as though *all of time existed simultaneously.* I was able to see what I perceived as my past lives and my future. I was able to see them all at the same time as though they were existing all at once.

I use a metaphor to help understand time. Imagine a huge tapestry with a beautiful intricate picture. If you were to go very close to the tapestry, almost to the point where your nose is touching it, you can't see the whole picture anymore. But you can see that the tapestry is woven with many individual strands of thread. My life is like one of those threads.

If I were to follow that strand, I would be living my life one point of time at a time. And as my thread weaves through the tapestry, it touches other threads or lives of others. It just keeps going—I may die, I may come back again—but that thread keeps going, just like my consciousness. But if I would step back, then I could see all the threads, I could see all the parts of my life at once. I could see the whole picture that it weaves as I touch other people and those people touch other people.

If I experience my life from just one point on that at a time, I could only see it as linear. But being in my NDE state was like I popped out of this life and saw an overview. *I could see the whole thing at the same time* including how all the other lives come together to create this beautiful, perfect tapestry that just makes sense.

P.M.H. ATWATER

It's just a walk through a doorway or shift in consciousness. It's simple. Every single person who has nearly died and come back says the same thing.

There are lots of things you can do, people you can meet, seeing loved ones who died including pets.

MARK PITSTICK

First, you don't really die. No one actually dies, it just appears that way. Remember that your human senses perceive much less than one percent of reality. When your body dies, it looks like that's the end when, in fact, it couldn't be further from the truth. Think back to a coat you wore when you were five years old. At some point you outgrew it and didn't need it anymore. That's basically what your human body is, an overcoat.

Your body is also like a car that takes you from womb to tomb. As many cultures recognize, when your soul is ready to graduate, you no longer need the bodily vehicle. In India, another term for dying is "dropping the body." A Native American term for death is "changing worlds." These are much more accurate descriptions of what really happens at death.

The next part of the question is, "After your real self discards the body, what will the next page in your life's eternal saga be like?" The answer is that *it depends on your level of consciousness at the time of your passing*. You've probably heard the saying, "You can't take it with you." That's true for your body and all your material possessions. What you do take with you, however, is *who you are*, your degree of love and realization. Heaven/ the Other Side isn't the same for everyone. There are probably as many versions of the next life as there are in this one.

While living on Earth, your outlook and attitude shape the quality of your experiences. Likewise, after you pass on, your level of energy/awareness influences what you experience in your next phase of forever. And, just as on Earth, the quality of your afterlife experience is not set in stone. Whenever you're ready, you can always upgrade the condition of your life at any time.

I use two extreme examples to help people understand the spectrum of potential experiences when somebody crosses over. The saintly nun Mother Teresa, for example, served many suffering people during her life and knew she was serving God in various distressful disguises. When she passed on, it was probably much like walking from one room to the other and being greeted by loved ones: "Bravo, Teresa! Welcome back home. After you rest up a bit, we could use your help with some important projects: souls who need healing, planets that need wise teachings, galaxies that are ready for peace." For her, dying was likely *a seamless transition* into the next part of life.

For Hitler, it probably was a different story. His decisions resulted in so many people suffering so horribly. He won't experience a fiery eternal hell, but he likely will experience a long, *self-induced hell* that could seem like eternity. Someone like Hitler would have to sleep for a long, long time because he couldn't bear to glimpse the effects of what he did.

Near-death experiencers tell about having a life review and consider it one of the most transformative aspects of the NDE. Ancient Aramaic and Hebrew words for heaven and hell meant, in part, 'How you feel after you die and you go through a passageway. You experience *a sorting out*, a review of all the good and bad you did, and feel the effects of your actions upon others.' Again, as you review your life, you not only watch it, you also *feel* the ripples that you created and how they impacted others.

So, in all likelihood, someone like Hitler couldn't initially stand the life review. That would begin only after a long period of sleep, counseling, and healing. Much about him that was evil and imbalanced would have to be burned away before his soul could be around others again. That's what teachings of hell-fires were about: burning away the old and lower energies until only pure soul, energy and consciousness is left.

You go through this process while on Earth; that's part of the value of a human incarnation. Your afterlife can be heavenly if you've burned away negativity and released dirty laundry from your earthly life. If you don't, it can be hellish for a while, but just for a while—not forever. Eternity is a very long time.

Parenthetically, Hitler was brutally abused as a child and obviously suffered an imbalanced mental state afterwards. So I can't say with certainty how much the Light takes all this into account. I do believe, based upon the evidence, that the Presence will welcome him Home—just like the Prodigal Son story in *The Bible*—when his soul is ready. But it could be a long time before Hitler's soul works through the self-loathing and guilt that inevitably arise from such evil actions.

MARILYN SCHLITZ

I have been very interested in consciousness studies and have looked at it through a variety of different methods. I started as an experimental parapsychologist looking at the idea that our consciousness may have the capacity to reach out and extend beyond our physical being. We designed experimental protocols in the laboratory using randomized, double-blind conditions that allowed us to document the possibility that one person's intention can seemingly reach out and cause physiological changes in another person. This suggests that there's something about our consciousness that is beyond the body.

I then started doing research and, for about 20 years, while at the Institute of Noetic Sciences, I've been looking at the nature of worldview transformation. We collected stories from people about their own transformative process: what catalyzed it, what sustained it, and what did it lead to? We interviewed sixty masters from different world traditions. We surveyed about 2,000 average people and compared what happened to them versus those who dropped out and lived in a cave. We talk about this work in our book, *Living Deeply: The Art and Science of Transformation in Everyday Life (Schlitz, Vieten and Amorok, 2007)*.

From all of that, my colleagues and I created *a change model*. One of the big factors in transformation is the relationship to death, what happens after death, and what is the meaning system we place on it. What we found is that there is a huge denial around death. The fear—terror actually—around mortality leads to a lot of aberrant behaviors, intolerance and aggression toward others, as well as distress for ourselves and other people. Many people ask the question, "What happens after I die?" There are many different answers.

For the last three years, I've been making the film *Death Makes Life Possible* and writing a book by the same title. I've interviewed people who represented different worldviews and models about the afterlife. We found a wide variety of answers to the question about an afterlife: everything from those who believe there's nothing after they die to those who have very sophisticated cosmologies. Buddhist traditions, for example, describe different spheres or "bardos" that we move through as we reach our next stage of consciousness journey. So there are a lot of different answers from different cultures and religions.

There are also ways in which science is attempting to answer that question. In the film and book, I explore the study of mediumship, for example. This involves people who believe they can channel discarnate entities, the personality of deceased persons. Scientists at IONS have been looking at what happens in the mediums' brains. Does something happen in their brains that's different when they believe they are in contact with spirits as compared to when they don't? It does appear that during these periods where the medium seems to be in contact with a personality, the memory center of the brain opens up. It appears as though the brain is creating a space for a different memory system to come in. That's all very preliminary, but interesting.

There's also fascinating work being done at the University of Virginia on reincarnation. It's documenting thousands of cases of people who have evidence that supports their belief that they were somebody in the past life. We're trying to systematically explore these things in different ways:

1. Basic science work that suggests consciousness is more than just our physical being;

2. Cultural perspectives that support the idea there's something more to us than our physicality;

3. What science is beginning to tell us about the nature of our transcendent capacities.

It's an exciting time where these different truth systems are coming together. For me personally, there's no one right answer. As an anthropologist, I really think that we each have to come up with an understanding of who we are, what our purposes are, and what's going to happen after death for ourselves in the context of our culture and families. Then, as we engage those questions, life fills in and gives us different possibilities.

GARY SCHWARTZ

The word death is no longer appropriate. There is no death for the being. There is transformation. There is "moving" to other dimensions. The word "death" is like the phrase "the sun revolves around the earth." It's just not that way.

When the physical body dies, our energy, information, memories, all of our history continues in the "vacuum of space" since everything that ever happened is present there. This is just slightly rephrasing what contemporary physics tell us and this is somewhat controversial.

The question is what do we do with all that energy and information? What do we do with our life experiences? There's scientific research that says a few different things can happen. Number one, people can "reincarnate." There's evidence from research at the University of Virginia, very strong evidence that supports the hypothesis that we can return to earth and continue to grow and be of service.

In addition, some people can choose to continue to be of service, but not necessarily reincarnate. In fact, the most exciting part of our current research is that we've been working on technology to detect the presence of spirits with what I call *a soul phone*. We're evolving from the cell phone to smart-phone to "soul phone."

In principle, and I describe this research in my book *The Sacred Promise*, it's only a matter of time before we're able to use technology to communicate with people who have "died", that is, people who have transitioned from life on earth. And then the love that they had while on earth can be sustained and evolved with people they knew and those they've never met.

The subtitle to that book is *How Science Is Discovering Spirit's Collaboration with Us in Our Daily Lives*. It discusses the whole notion of other potential roles for departed souls. They don't have to come back to the earth in a physical form but they can continue to have relationships with their children or their grandchildren. And they can help care for the planet because they love earth and wish to be of service. Then there's all the freedom once you lose your physical body: you can go to other places in the universe and potentially to other universes. You can better know the Source. There are lots of opportunities.

My personal opinion is that we have choice in our after-death possibilities. There's choice at every level. We also have responsibility and soul contracts. You know the phrase, "As above, so below." Well, there are also indications that "As below, so above" is true. I think the notion of our choosing and fulfilling different missions is a very plausible one.

CAROLINE MYSS

Who knows? The one thing I'm sure of is we go on. After that, we make most of it up. We don't have our theologies straight to start with. We have earth-centric religions when we should have universal theologies since there's life everywhere in the universe. So from the get-go, our theologies are askew. We have Gods that look like us when, in fact, Gods don't look like us. So our mythologies are elementary. Do we go on after this life? The likelihood is, absolutely. Do I have any idea what that's like? No.

What I gather from near-death experiences is we are greeted by souls who have gone on before, who are familiar to us. It also seems consistent that the afterlife realm is infinitely loving and beautiful. Another common report is that there is a life review, being held accountable for actions in which we withheld choices we could've made that were more benevolent, more unselfish, and more loving. Those choices would have made a tremendous difference in the lives of others and we are given an opportunity to see the impact those choices would have had. That's fairly profound.

BILL GUGGENHEIM

I don't know if there's so much a difference of where they go according to how they live their life. We like to think that the good guys go this way and the bad guys go that way. But I think those are earth standards. Near-death experiences provide a good model for what it's like to die, but it doesn't necessarily have to occur that way. We probably do go through something like a tunnel and perhaps into the Light where we feel a sense of returning home. We do have reunions with our deceased loved ones.

But in order to feel we are really in heaven, it has to align with our consciousness. If someone's a Protestant and they wind up in a Catholic heaven, they're not going to feel they're in heaven. They're not where they want to be and it wouldn't be heavenly for them. Same thing if someone was a Buddhist and wound up in a Hindu heaven. That wouldn't work for them. Heaven has to be a place that's aligned with our own values system and way of thinking.

In the same way, if someone was a criminal and was very malicious to other people, they will go to a level where they feel comfortable. Others around them will be of a like mind. This doesn't mean they're being punished. It's not about judgment. It's about *like finding like* and seeking its own level.

However, they will have infinite opportunities to elevate their consciousness. They can always grow to higher spiritual levels, but they have to desire to do so. If people in wars killed civilians and did unspeakable crimes, they think what they did was right and won't ask for help. But if their level of afterlife is like that for a long time, they may change their minds and want out of it. They may ask for help to reach a higher level and move on. Angels, spiritual teachers, whatever you call them, are always available to assist their evolution. Eventually, those people can come back to earth school and really prove they have changed by living it.

Now, some people might say, "That sounds awfully easy on the bad guys like Hitler, Mussolini and so on." It's easy to single out Hitler, but to my knowledge, he himself never took a gun and killed anybody. Now, I'm not going to say he wasn't a mad man. His words and decisions killed millions and millions of people and caused immense suffering and hardship.

But the people who followed him are also responsible for all that death and suffering. It took all those followers to carry out his orders. They bear responsibility just as much as he does for the atrocities to the Jews, Gypsies and others around the world.

At the same time, all that death and suffering allowed many other people to be good guys and for humanity to learn important lessons. So in a broad sense—if no one really dies except on the earthly level and we all survive it—perhaps we chose these horrors.

BERNIE SIEGEL

What happens? Your body dies, your consciousness does not. When you leave your body, you don't take any afflictions or problems with you, just your consciousness. People who were born blind and have a near-death experience see again when they are out of their body. How do you think and how do you see when you are not in your body anymore? Those are things I was not having trouble doing as a child when I watched myself choking to death on a toy.

So you die in the sense that your body does, but your conscious doesn't. It can go on and improve the world or make it worse. If you are bitter, resentful, and hateful, you might impact others that way. But what if you bring them the experience that says we need to love the world, befriend each other, help each other?

STAN GROF

I had a very strict methodistic upbringing. I studied medicine in Prague when we had a Marxist regime and were controlled by the Soviet Union. So I got the purest naturalistic education you can get: we are our bodies and consciousness is the product of the brain; when the body dies, the brain dies and that's the end of the story.

I think in a much more complicated way after fifty years of studying consciousness. We now have a whole new discipline that started in the late 60's. Thanatology is the study of people who had near-death experiences and those who approached death.

We have reports from people who went quite far on that journey. After they were resuscitated, a significant number of them reported quite fantastic adventures. They relived their whole lives within a very short period of time. They had experiences of passing through a tunnel and confronting the Divine Light, God. They looked at their life and evaluated it. They reached a certain point that they felt was a point of no return.

Now, we don't have stories of people who experienced the full extent of dying because they returned. But they went far enough to confirm some of the reports that we find in the *Tibetan and Egyptian Books of the Dead* and *Ars Moriendi, The Art of Dying* from the European tradition.

Based on all that, I believe that death is going to be a fantastic journey. It's not going to be just having your light switched off.

KAREN WYATT

My answers are based on what I have experienced with patients and what I have understood through my own life experiences. At the time of death, the soul leaves the body. On several occasions, I have witnessed the soul of a patient actually leaving the body. I then observed the body gradually declining and dying for thirty minutes or so afterwards.

The soul leaves the body and the body is given back to the earth. It returns to the elements of the earth because it's no longer needed. Then the soul merges back into the spiritual realm where the soul really has its home. This is where the soul has connection and is part of a vast matrix of energy and power.

MARK ANTHONY

I think the possibilities are beyond our finite understanding, but that doesn't mean we can't try. What happens when we die? The first line of my book *Never Letting Go* is, "When you die, you really don't." Physical existence may end, but the physical part of us is just an infinitesimally small sub-fraction of what we really are. When we leave our body, we revert to an immortal consciousness.

Here's the best way I can describe it using earthly terms to explain an infinite concept. Every soul is like a drop of water that is pure consciousness. When we leave the body, that drop plunges into the infinite ocean on the Other Side. Our souls are connected to everything and everyone—everywhere. However, we can assume our individuality because that's one of the gifts from God. Our individuality can separate from the collective consciousness when we need to. It can detach when we want to communicate with those who are living in the material world.

The spectrum of possibilities when a person passes on is infinite. A lot of people have contacted me about loved ones who committed suicide. In traditional Judaism, Christianity and Islam, those who commit suicide go to Hell. People are just devastated at the thought of a loved one in torment forever. In my next book Evidence of Eternity, I spend a lot of time discussing suicide and I can tell you this, there is no "one size fits all."

We are all children of God, God being the most loving parent of all. No good earthly parent would ever condemn a child to an eternity of suffering. That doesn't mean there are not repercussions for our behaviors. But this Bronze Age idea of being cast into the pit of fire forever? I don't mean to offend anyone, but that's just primitive nonsense. *(Mark Anthony, the Psychic Lawyer, author of Never Letting Go and Evidence of Eternity)*

RAYMOND MOODY

The idea of an afterlife has never set well with me, it just seemed counter-intuitive. But recently, I've sort of woken up and run out of other options about that one. So, oddly enough, I think there is—in addition to this vast life—another one that somehow encompasses the immensity of life. I can't come up with an alternate frame of reference to account for all this except to say I think there is an afterlife.

4 IS THERE A GOD/ HIGHER POWER/ SOURCE?

IF SO, WHAT IS THAT PHENOMENON LIKE AND WHAT IS OUR RELATIONSHIP TO IT?

ANITA MOORJANI

Yes, there is a God. I feel that a lot our problems on earth are caused because we feel separate from God. It's that conditioned belief or feeling of separation that often causes suffering within us. We feel God is a separate entity who judges and punishes us so we're constantly thinking of how do I get God to favor me.

When I was in the NDE state, I felt as though I became God or I became one with God. We are all one with God all the time, there is no separation. There's no difference between me and God. There's no difference between you and God.

Others may judge you if you say that, but when I look in the mirror, I realize it's God reflecting Itself behind my eyes and experiencing Itself through my body. When I remember that, it becomes easier for me to see God behind your eyes and behind everyone's eyes. As more people realize this, crime and other forms of suffering will decrease. When people realize they are part of God and everyone else is too, they are less likely to harm other people.

P.M.H. ATWATER

Yes, but it's not a person, place or thing. It's not a man or a woman, and it's not God sitting on a throne so let's do away with all of that stuff. That Source that we come from, that intelligence, is so beyond any words we can use. How do you describe that? All of the near-death experiencers face the same dilemma. It's not just an energy, ectoplasm, or spirit. It's beyond all of that. It's beyond anything you can imagine. Today, I no longer believe in God, I know God. I breathe God. God is my every breath.

Look at all our religions, spiritual teachers, mediums, and people who nearly died. God is bigger than what they describe and it's because our language can't define the Light. We can't say in words what It is because we don't have the words.

The Light is greater than the light of 10,000 suns, so we're not speaking about a yard light here. It's a Light that knows your name, knows all about you, and can converse with you.

When I died the third time, I was greeted by a voice. I call it "the voice like none other." It was the kind of voice that speaks with thunder and was so powerful. It was beyond powerful.

Yes, BUT God is not a big guy in the sky and is certainly not just a "He." God is beyond gender, thus the more appropriate pronoun usage 'It.' Or, if that sounds too impersonal to you, alternately use He, She or It. In the Aramaic language commonly spoken at the time of Jesus, the word for the Source meant, in part, "unity consciousness." The English word for God came from the same German root word as 'good.' These are different facets of the Creator, a phenomenon that is much more complex and vast than "He."

There have been various names from different cultures for the creative power and intelligence that imbues all life. To name just a few: Great Spirit from Native Americans, All That Is from Middle Eastern cultures, and the Ground of All Being from more contemporary thinkers. People who have near-death experiences often use the terms 'the Light' and 'the Presence' to describe this background energy that is always everywhere. They say we each are like passengers on a train and God is powering the train.

I hate to say it, but I think the *Star Wars* movies have done a better job depicting the God phenomena than a lot of religions have. Their salutation "May The Force be with you" rings more true with modern day spiritual seekers than do limiting archaic images.

Realizing our interconnectedness with, rather than separation from, the Divine is a key to personal and planetary harmony. How many generations have tried to wrap their heads around schizophrenic teachings about a God of love who would send any of His creation to a fiery hell forever?

The good news is we each are one with the One *right now*—not maybe, someday, if we do certain things or believe a certain way. It's a wonderful set up.

Maybe I have a complicated worldview, but it holds that there are a multiplicity of perspectives that exist simultaneously. I don't have a final trump card that I think is the answer. I'm really much more interested in what are the questions we can ask that are revealed through mystical experiences that people report.

One of the people I interviewed is an Imam for the Sufi tradition. As a teenager growing up in Morocco, he was floating on the water and suddenly had an experience that his body grew bigger and bigger. Finally, he had that kind of unitive, mystical, samadhi-type experience that people describe. This sense of his own connection to Allah or the One in his tradition really informed the rest of his life.

The whole transformation research project began one day when a very successful business man, Jewish by upbringing but pretty secular, had one of these opening experiences that gave him insight into the Divine and he wanted to understand it. He came to my office and said, "Tell me what the research says. Do a lot of people have these experiences and if they do, what can we learn? And if they don't, how can we help them to have them because they really are great."

We started doing research and the literature basically said, "People who have these mystical opening experiences are either delusional or psychotic." But that was not what we were hearing from people. The scientific and psychological literature had some questions about these mystical, spiritual, and religious experiences. In the twenty years since we started working on that project, things have changed so much. I just saw a new study that's being done looking at the differences between religion and spirituality in terms of how people answer the questions that you're asking. They were basically saying that religion provides a set of rules and boundaries whereas spirituality provides an opening to ask questions and experience our sense of oneness with whatever we put a name on.

There are lots of answers to the questions, "What is the divine? Is there a God?" Is it one God, is it personified in some form, or is it really something that we have no language to describe?" And yet, we get glimpses into all this when we have opening experiences. People do things like walk in nature and, if it's done with intention and attention, it can be revelatory and people can really feel grace. The same with the meditation state when people sit down and get themselves into a deep mindfulness state or a contemplative prayer type state. There are glimpses and openings for people to find whatever the answer is for them about this question. It's a beautiful inquiry.

GARY SCHWARTZ

In the book I wrote called *The G.O.D. Experiments*, I used the subtitle *How Science Is Discovering God in Everything—Including Us*. The word "small" has the word "all" in it and, literally, the All is in the small. A hologram can have stores of information of everything in it and that everything can be simultaneously present everywhere. The notion is that there's this infinite potential, what David Bohm called the implicate order, this consciousness, intelligence, universal mind, universal source in everything. And it has the capacity to be manifest in a zillion number of ways including in the form of a human.

From this point of view, this universal consciousness or source energy would be in everything. And we can consciously access it, make requests of it, and be of service to it in an intentional way.

For me, one of the most fascinating things about the Source is the more we live a life of love, compassion, and caring, the more we have the capacity to be in harmony with and experience what Larry Dossey calls the One Mind. One of the ways that expresses itself is in *synchronicity*. The more one chooses to live in harmony and with the highest intentions, the more one will see evidence of, as my wife Wanda calls it, the continuity of encouragement. You see not just subtle signs of interconnections between things, but ever more evidence of the nonrandom nature of the universe being expressed in our daily lives.

CAROLINE MYSS

To me, God is law and that's it. If you want to understand the nature of God or the Divine, it is mystical law. Law is consistent, and mystical laws are fully and totally evident. All that exists is subject to the nature of the mystical laws and, as they incarnate, they become the physical laws of science. All that exists is subjected to law and that's the nature of God. You can trust the nature of the Tao, the great way.

When you extend too much into negativity, something will collapse in you that brings about a forced reboot in order for you to survive. And in that reboot, you will become more conscious one way or another and that is how negativity forces an awakening.

When you abuse your body, you will go into illness. That's just the law. You've broken the laws of health. It's not a punishment, it's simply the law. That's why all the great teachers, what did they teach? They taught law. Jesus was a great teacher of the laws of healing.

Now, the way in which the laws become personal, the way in which you come to know the nature of God, is through prayer. Prayer is how the laws begin to pulsate within you and the miracle is when God bends the mystical laws just for you. Mystical laws are fluid and are managed by grace. That's the nature of the Divine; it is a breathing, unified field of grace.

But once the laws become solid in the field of physical matter, they can't be changed. If you drop something, all the prayers in the world are not going to stop gravity from operating. You can pray until the cows come home, but you're not going to suspend that object in midair. But you'll get Divine intervention if you pray, "Do not let my thoughts become so grave that they affect my life." That's the nature of God. It's not an off-planet creature with a beard that fills your Christmas basket. Nothing could be more ridiculous.

BILL GUGGENHEIM

I believe very much that there's a higher power, a source, a creator. For me, it's one word: LOVE. When we slow 'love' down in vibration or frequency, it becomes light. And when you slow 'light' down in vibration or frequency, it becomes energy and when you slow 'energy' down, it becomes matter. Going in reverse: matter, energy, light, love. I don't think of Creator as being a person or looking like a person although it could if It wanted to. It created all that is and is all there is. Everything throughout the universe is God and everything beyond that.

We think of artists and their paintings, or sculptors and their pottery, as being separate. One created the other. But the Creator of all life is not separate from Its creation. It's part of that creation as well. It's not duality, but oneness. And that's why saints and others are in bliss. They are truly tuned into theoneness of all creation that is infinite love or God.

BERNIE SIEGEL

God is not a person. My definition of God is loving, intelligent, conscious energy. Those are the things that you need to create and sustain a universe.

STAN GROF

In my book *The Cosmic Game*, I asked the question, "If this is a journey of spiritual discovery, when do people feel they've actually found what they are looking for?" I found two experiences where people felt they had reached the Ultimate. One of them saw an incredibly intense source of light, like millions of suns, but there was also intelligence, creativity, even a sense of humor. The insight was that this is where creation comes from, this is the principle that creates the phenomenal world.

Another person felt he had reached the source of creation. Paradoxically, the experience was of a void, a kind of meta-cosmic, supra-cosmic emptiness that is conscious of itself. Although there are no concrete forms, this void actually contains all creation in a potential form. These descriptions are parallel to what you can find in modern physics, for example, in the work of Ervin László.

KAREN WYATT

Yes, absolutely. The God that I am aware of is the source of all creation. God is pure creative energy which is love. Creator breathes everything into existence, every form of matter and energy. God also instills everything with an impulse to grow, create, achieve maximum diversity, and explore all possibilities.

We each have within us a divine spark. This divine impulse urges us to keep growing, evolve, and expand our potentials. It wants us to become the highest beings that we are capable of becoming—as souls and as human beings here on the planet. We possess that spark, that creative energy that comes from God, as we live on Earth. Beyond that, God is also a mystery and is unknown in many ways.

MARK ANTHONY

Absolutely, God exists. And God exists in spite of religion, not because of religion. Even though I refer to religions as being myth and fear-based, they do serve a tremendous purpose. I like what Pope Francis has been saying. He's not out to change or indoctrinate people or make them believe differently than what they do. I believe that religion is a good path for connecting with God as long as it is not used to justify or promote anger, fear, bigotry, hatred or violence. That is when any connection with God seizes to exist.

God has a multitude of names: Source, Spirit, Vishnu, Jehovah, Allah, Yeshua, Great Spirit, and so on. God is the source of all light, power, love, creativity, energy, and intelligence in the universe. God is a spiritual being that is multi-dimensional and transcends all space and time. Everything is connected to God; that's how Spirit is aware of what's happening everywhere at all times. The Source is, in one sense, so far beyond our comprehension and yet so easy to grasp. I love what the Hindus say, 'God is love. When you look into the eyes of someone you love, and who truly loves you, you're catching but a glimpse of God.'

We're all part of Spirit, we're like cells in the body of God. We're all created in the image of God who is a spiritual being, ergo, we are spiritual beings and are interconnected with all life. *(Mark Anthony, the Psychic Lawyer, author of Never Letting Go and Evidence of Eternity)*

RAYMOND MOODY

God is a reality that's far more vast than any human concept. To me, God is about relationships—with you personally and your ones with other people too. God is watching everything through everybody's eyes, not just over this human existence but over the entire cosmos. I can say I have a personal relationship with God. Relationships with God are a lifelong development that change as you grow older and go through different stages in life.

Prayer kind of keeps me going, and I don't mean "Oh God, give me a color TV" and I don't mean "Please save the world." My prayers are very minimal, basically prayers for my children because they are still young. I figure that things beyond that are not any of my business. I wouldn't pray, "Oh please, don't let G.E. stock go down." The bigger plan, God's plot, is much better than this drama that we are in, than any other solution I can come up with. Surrender is the most powerful prayer: let it be worked out. That always ends up being the best solution.

5 WHY IS THERE SO MUCH SUFFERING?

THIS ISSUE IS ESPECIALLY DIFFICULT TO UNDERSTAND WHEN CHILDREN SUFFER AND DIE.

ANITA MOORJANI

When a little child or anyone dies, it's the people around them who suffer; the deceased has gone Home. We die when it's our time to die and, even when a child dies, that happens at the perfect time. The child came here for a short while and presented gifts to many people and then it's time for the child to go Home. The timing was most likely determined before the child came to earth. So there's one form of what we label as suffering, but if we viewed it differently, we would not see it as suffering. We would be happy for our time with that child and know that he or she is now safe and back Home.

There are several reasons why children suffer with illness. It could be part of the soul's plan since, very often, illness brings gifts to others and brings people closer. Another type of suffering is what is I called *senseless suffering* which we bring upon ourselves because of our conditioning. We may have been taught that we're separate, we have to be more than who we are and be more competitive. Feeling that we're not good enough weakens our immune systems and causes many other problems. So that's a kind of suffering we bring on ourselves and we have a choice to not do that.

Before my NDE, I suffered a lot. I made myself small so others could feel big and I lived from a place of fear. I feared illness, not being good enough, I was a people pleaser. Everything I did and every decision I made came from a place of fear. That contributed to my suffering and to getting cancer.

When I was in that near death state, the clarity was so incredible that I was not supposed to live in fear. I was supposed to make my choices out of love and passion and I wasn't supposed to be suffering. And what I felt was, "Why didn't I know this before? Why aren't we taught this as children?" That's when I realized that most of our suffering comes from being conditioned to believe in and do the wrong things.

The biggest thing I learned was that the most important thing I can do is to love and value myself. The more we love and value ourselves, the less we suffer. A lot of suffering stems from devaluing ourselves and thinking that we don't matter.

Another big thing I learned was to *make choices from a place of love instead of a place of fear*. Before my NDE, I was obsessive about being healthy. I used to research anticancer products and lifestyles. I ate healthfully, took all my supplements, drank wheat grass juice, and guess what? I got cancer. During my NDE, I understood that was because everything I did in my life was from a place of fear.

Today I still choose healthy foods, but I do it not because I'm obsessive about cancer. I do it because I love my life. I'm passionate about my life

---

and consciously choose what brings me love and joy instead of fearing the consequences. I don't suffer anymore. Life is so much more pleasant, so much more fun.

P.M.H. ATWATER

That's by our choice on a soul level. From the greater perspective of I AM consciousness, there seems to be purpose and direction in suffering. One man I met was wheelchair bound and had a chronic disease, but said very calmly with a smile on his face, "I have the privilege to be in this body to teach people that there really is such a thing as courage."

I was born illegitimate; I have five fathers, two mothers, and I wound up raising myself. I had polio, St. Vitus Dance, rheumatic fever, synesthesia, and dyslexia at a time when school systems never even heard of it. My experience of first grade was a horrible, horrible nightmare. I spent most of it on a stool in front of the class wearing a tall conical hat that said "Dunce" on it. I wasn't tortured physically. I was tortured mentally.

Despite all that and much more, I wouldn't change a thing. I had a moment on a sheer rock ledge overlooking Shoshone Falls. I'm all by myself and looking over the falls and suddenly all of the people in my life since birth stood there: the people who hurt me, those who who tortured me in one way or another, the people I loved and who saved me… all of them were there. I realized that it was all part of a plan, it was all part of a miracle. It was all part of what enabled me to be the person I am today and I look back at them and smile and thank God.

Why would a soul come in as a child and pass on at a very early age in earth years? In my research base of 277 children, half of them could clearly remember their birth and 1/3 could remember pre-birth going back seven months in-utero. So we're talking about souls who are fully aware of the process, who are fully aware of what they're coming into. We hear, again and again in the near-death research, that a soul knows why it's here. It knew the big picture even as its spark was vitalizing the cells in its little body inside the mother's womb.

MARK PITSTICK

I've been with children as they died from abuse or severe injuries in hospitals and counseled many parents whose children have died. I've worked with tens of thousands of suffering patients in the last forty years. Personally, I've had loved ones die, divorce, heart breaks, financial losses, big disappointments, etc. So I know, personally and professionally, that suffering and death—particularly involving children—can be very difficult.

Change and challenge are part of life. Knowing the afterlife evidence doesn't take away all the pain from death and suffering, but it does lighten it. For example, there's a huge difference between believing death is a good-bye versus a "see you later." You can better handle life's challenges when you know there are greater meanings and purposes involved.

That's why I do everything I can to share the *documented clinical and scientific evidence* that clearly shows no one really dies. This information also indicates that life is purposeful and fair—not chaotic and cruel. When you really internalize this great news, your level of fear about any part of life—including suffering and death—diminishes.

Native Americans did not have a word for the concept of fear. They knew that life is a day-to-day walk through eternity with Great Spirit. 'What of any lasting importance—paralysis, loss of limb, death—can go wrong since we are walking hand-in-hand with Wakan Tanka?' they asked. When you really understand that life is never-ending—even though it often changes—your suffering decreases. Yes, you may feel sad and grieve some for a while, but not nearly to the extent you would if you didn't have a spiritual foundation and greater understanding of how life unfolds.

One cause of suffering is an over-identification with aspects of your earthly life that change. For example, if you excessively focus on your body, beauty, and youth, you are setting yourself up to suffer because you will eventually lose everything about yourself that you can see. It's OK *to prefer* to be healthy and youthful, but it's important to have peace when those slip away.

It's important to primarily identify with your timeless nature, your spirit, consciousness, love. Those things don't go away or die.

The Buddha was reportedly asked, "Why is there suffering?" He said for two reasons:

1. *Growth opportunities* – suffering provides fertile ground for learning and expanding. When you are hurting, you are more motivated to seek sensible answers to life's toughest questions. That enables you to reach down deep, realize just how strong and wise you are, and grow.

2. *Service opportunities* – one of the people we interviewed in the *Soul Proof* movie had a child die from brain cancer. When he and his wife visited her in the cancer ward, they would often find her visiting and reassuring other pediatric and even adult patients. Her suffering allowed her to serve others in ways not possible if she were healthy.

It's very difficult when a child dies. But it's important to consider that, even though a child might be young in earth years, she is probably an evolved soul. As such, she didn't need to take a long earthly curriculum. Nearly all bereaved parents I've ever worked with described their deceased child as a special and sensitive person. They often feared that their children would die at a young age because they seemed too good for this world.

It's also important to remember that, whether a person is five or ninety-five years-old when he passes on, that those years are just a blink of an eye in the span of eternity. Again, purported teachings of the Buddha are instructive in this matter: 'You want to know what a human incarnation is like? Look at ocean waves breaking and the drops of water that shoot up into the air for a moment and then fall back into the water. That's how transient a human life is.' This perspective helps us realize how time-limited suffering really is.

Would you hang by your thumbs for five minutes to save a child's life? Of course you would. Well, human suffering is very similar: it's very brief in the span of eternity, can have great purpose, and is well worth it from a cosmic perspective.

Finally, it's important to consider that you, as a soul, *volunteered* to go through tough times. It makes a big difference if suffering is your choice and not arbitrarily forced upon you by a dictatorial God.

Do what you can to minimize suffering, but when you're faced with it, embrace, honor, bless, and learn from it. This approach lightens and enlightens your earth-experience—even the sad and bad parts. Remember that any good story has bad guys and struggle so the heroes/heroines can grow and realize their inner potentials. And your earth-experience is, among other things, a great story.

MARILYN SCHLITZ

Well, I can say for sure it's real and that people suffer. I worked at the Institute of Noetic Sciences with the founder Dr. Edgar Mitchell who was one of the Apollo 14 astronauts. He had the opportunity to walk on the moon and then, because his part of the mission was complete, had the window seat on the way home. He was able to look out that little portal as they blasted through space and watched the sun, the moon, and the earth, rising and setting. He was able to see what is now a common image of our pristine planet suspended in the vastness of space and see all of its perfection.

He had two responses or experiences. One was deep suffering as he really felt the pain of our planet. But as he looked at Earth in all of its wholeness, he didn't see national boundaries, state boundaries, race boundaries, ethnic boundaries, gender boundaries, age boundaries . . . he didn't see any of that. He just thought that it was something whole and beautiful. So suffering isn't something inherent in the planet, it's really inherent in the inhabitants of planet earth.

We are *meaning-making creatures* who define suffering with certain values and judgment. In part, suffering comes from a natural developmental response to things that happen in our lives. It also comes from our worldview and where we place our attention. Personally, I think there's every reason to believe that we stay connected. It's just defining that connection in a different form.

Going back to scientific research, it had been thought that people are usually incapacitated by profound experiences of suffering such as the death of a child or loved one. These things are big in our life, but what we're discovering is that people by and large are more resilient than we first thought. It's important to be aware of our resilience, to be aware of the gift of life, to understand that grief is a process. It comes and then we move through it—not ever forgetting, but redefining.

There are tools that can help people overcome grief, to live through it and get back to life. Personal tools for processing grief include gratefulness meditation and having appreciation for a loving relationship that can cause such deep grief. Other ways include walking in a labyrinth, seated meditation, contemplative prayers, journaling, creative expression, and arts. We can pay attention to dreams where we sense our loved ones who have died and feel we are with them in some way. Those can be very exhilarating for people and can give them a tangible feeling of connections to their departed. I discuss death dreams in my book, *Death Makes Life Possible.*

Then there are *collective practices* that we can do. The Day of the Dead ceremonies in Latin America are based on the belief that the veil between the living and the dead becomes thin at that time of year and there's more access to communications with the departed. People make little altars, offer food and drink, and put up pictures so they can talk to their deceased loved ones. There is a direct communication and no sense that the departed person is very far away and separate.

Other cultures have celebrations like the Irish Wake. Other traditions like the Celts have a philosophy of honoring the dead because they are here, they're with us and in us. It's sad when a loved one dies, but it's also a time to honor and celebrate their lives. It's also a time to look at our lives and consider what it means to be alive. That's ultimately the gift and the opportunity in this process of contemplating mortality.

GARY SCHWARTZ

Of course, it's a fundamental question. There are multiple reasons for what we call suffering. Number one is protection. For example, as young children, we learn to not put our hands in fire so we don't get burned. How do we know not to put our hands in fire? Because we experience pain. Pain is a built-in mechanism and its purpose is to inform us when we injure ourselves and prevent future injuries. So, in that respect, pain as a built-in capacity for suffering is actually a gift. It's a gift because, without it, we would constantly be hurting ourselves.

Secondly, if we don't have the capacity for fear, we will not survive. Sometimes there are real dangers in the world and people who lose the capacity for fear are less likely to survive. So fear is also a gift. What about depression? Depression is also a gift because if we don't feel sadness, we will be less concerned about the people that we love. So our capacity to feel pain, fear, sadness, loss, and guilt provides us with feedback to love and care more, so these are not bad things per se.

Now the next question is why does disease occur? And, even worse, why do we do such cruel things to ourselves and others? The primary explanation I know is that one of the gifts humans are given is the gift of relative freedom. We are given the opportunity to make choices—including making mistakes—and to take responsibility. Expecting God to do things that we can do ourselves is missing the point. We want the freedom to be able to make choices. Everybody loves freedom, but with freedom comes responsibility.

The last thing is that some people come to Earth with designs for a shorter life. Their suffering from illness and/or an early death is not just for them personally. It's not that they are serving karma or penance to make up for mistakes they made in the past. There may also be an agreement that they come into life and suffer to help others learn compassion and take responsibility.

So there could be many levels of why suffering occurs. My conclusion is that the Source—that creates life and gives us freedom to grow, explore and make our own mistakes—has created a very wise and caring system.

CAROLINE MYSS

After all these years of closely working with many people, I have come to the conclusion that the majority of what people suffer is of their own making. There are sufferings that happen in life that appear to come out of the clear blue, but many are choices people make. Look at the tornadoes that hit the

Midwest. Many of those people were asked, "Weren't you supposed to put in shelters?" and they said, "We decided not to because blah, blah, blah."

The wise choices that are available to people are often not made. We are constantly standing at the crossroads of wisdom or woe. How often do we eat what we shouldn't? We say what we shouldn't to people. We think what we shouldn't. We make foolish choices. We overspend in the moment and then rationalize by saying we've had a bad day or a good day. We don't manage our bills properly. We don't manage life properly.

So why is there suffering? Because we choose foolish things, we do foolish things, and we do them again and again. We don't work our way through, we don't navigate our way out. All the spiritual teachers tell us vengeance is foolish and it won't accomplish anything, but we're still vengeful. We make choices that are not productive; we know that and we make them anyway. So we suffer.

Many people tell me, "I have a lot of fear. I can't move forward because of fear." So often, people want another person to make decisions for them because they're terrified of the consequence of the decision. I get that. As I told a woman recently, you're unhappy in the known. You might be unhappy in the unknown, but at least you have a chance for adventure and happiness. She's in the known and she's going to continue to suffer, but she'll stay there because she's more terrified to take a risk. So that's another reason why we suffer.

BILL GUGGENHEIM

Suffering is resistance to what is. Let's say I want a woman to be my girlfriend or wife, but she wants to end the relationship. I'm going to suffer if I'm holding on and resisting the flow of what somebody else wants.

I have a very good friend who is a social worker at a hospital and works with many children who have cancer. I've talked with her about these things and I think the children elected to develop cancer and experience it. Some will be healed, many will not be. Their parents will go through all the agony when their child dies. I know what it's like to lose a child.

But this is where the growth comes in even though it's as painful as hell. I won't deny that. Some of the most free and joyous people I have ever met are those who work with the terminally ill and others who are just there loving children and others unconditionally.

Compassionate Friends is another group that has moved me so deeply. It's the largest self-help group for bereaved parents. All of the chapter leaders and managers have had one or more children who died. Those people work through all that pain and suffering, and then are able to help others. These are some of the most loving, accepting, and compassionate people I've ever encountered.

BERNIE SIEGEL

A perfect world is not a creation, it's a magic trick. We are here to live and learn and having free will makes our actions meaningful. We are here to raise the level of consciousness so that someday we will have a world where love is shared by everyone. It will be free of suffering although pain is still necessary to protect us and make us aware of our feelings and relationships. Without pain, we would be in big trouble emotionally and physically. But with love and compassion, the pain is diminished and tolerable.

STAN GROF

Well, that's the most difficult question of them all. When you are on the spiritual journey and discover there is a divine principle, you ask "Why is there suffering?" I have a whole chapter in my book *The Cosmic Game* on good and evil. Ultimately, the idea is that if the Divine wants to get to know itself, it would be incomplete if it didn't include an awareness of the dark, of the shadows. Creation also requires polarity so that's another element.

When Ramakrishna was asked, "Why is there suffering in the world?" he gave a strange answer: "To thicken the plot." When I heard it, I thought "Why are you saying thicken the plot? Look at all the little children who are suffering and dying from cancer, killed in Syria or somewhere, or by napalm in Vietnam."

And then I started thinking about what would happen if we eliminated everything that we consider dark. *You would lose a big part of the story.* For example, eliminating disease would get rid of all the healers and good Samaritans like Mother Theresa. Ending war would also exclude all the heroes, inspiring stories like Tolstoy's *War and Peace*, war-inspired art and movies, and so on.

So if we removed all the things that are dark, you would get a very flat story. Then, inevitably, the next question arises, "Does it have to go that far? Can't we keep the polarity, but maintain reasonable limits?" This becomes a major challenge in our spiritual journeys—to embrace creation with its shadow side. All we can do is change the way we contribute to the world, to contribute more positive energy than participate in the shadow side.

KAREN WYATT

What I have witnessed—and I've had many opportunities to see and learn this—is that suffering is *part of the wisdom path* on this earthly plane. We, as souls, incarnate on earth—in part—to learn how to navigate through suffering. Suffering provides many important lessons that we can learn, for example, compassion and tolerance.

Our souls come here to experience suffering on different levels—physical, mental, emotional, spiritual—in order to learn the wisdom that suffering contains. By experiencing suffering on this planet, we are able to perfect our skills. Each lifetime gives us opportunities to develop living with intention, purpose and love. *Suffering brings us to the brink* so we are finally able to learn lessons that we need while we're on this planet.

Suffering opens us to learning love and forgiveness; it teaches us about surrender and impermanence. So suffering has a profound purpose for us. It is a tool that helps us fully manifest our purposes while on earth. It strips away what is false and leaves us as more authentic beings.

It can be very difficult to accept when children are suffering and dying. In my experiences of working with dying children through hospice, I have seen that many of them were highly developed souls... very highly evolved souls who came here for the purpose of helping their parents and others. So the child's illness and death were a voluntary sacrifice on that soul's part to provide learning and growth opportunities for the family and many others.

MARK ANTHONY

I remember the movie "Oh God" with George Burns who played God. John Denver asked him, "How can you permit all the suffering that goes on the world?" God looked at him and said, "How can I permit the suffering? I don't permit the suffering. You do. Free will. All the choices are yours. You can love each other, cherish and nurture each other or you can kill each other." Even though the movie was termed a comedy, there was so much in it that was incredibly profound.

The question invariably arises, "If God is love, then why do we have to endure all this suffering?" There is no eternal hell, but sometimes life on Earth is hellish. We each go through a succession of lifetimes in this material world.

When we've experienced what we wanted and balanced out our karma, there's no more need to return to this Earth plane with its inherent suffering.

I am not for one second downplaying the suffering of anyone. I look at people who have lost children, the strife and suffering in the Middle East, Crimea, North Korea, Africa and even in our own families. In the last week, my uncle died and then a few days later his son died in an accident. So within five days, my family sustained two terrible losses.

Perhaps these things happen to us so that we can grow. I firmly believe that we can grow the most when negative and painful things happen to us. It's a choice. When suffering strikes, I could become an alcoholic and engage in destructive behaviors. Or I could become a more understanding, compassionate, and wise person.

When children suffer, it's important to remember that even though a child might be young in Earth years, its soul is likely quite evolved.

During a reading when I connect with spirits on the other side, I sometimes see a bright star. That usually means the client had a child that died in utero or at a very young age. But communicating with the spirit of a fetus or very young child is not "Goo-goo, gaga." That entity is an immortal living spirit. It's amazing to see what souls know about the family that never got to know them. One time, I was doing a reading and the spirit of an unborn child started talking about a Mr. Coffee coffeemaker. The client said, "Oh my God, I bought one of those yesterday and I miscarried that child fifteen years ago." The spirit was letting her know he was aware of what was going on in her life. Even though he was not born into the physical world, he was still part of her life. *(Mark Anthony, the Psychic Lawyer, author of Never Letting Go and Evidence of Eternity)*

I wish there was more I could say and do to help when people suffer, especially when a child dies. My first child died in 1970 at the age of 36 hours and that is a terrible thing to this day. I know that feeling. That loss is always going to be there, but it has enabled me to counsel people who have been through a loss of a child. The pain is not going to get completely reconciled and yet your consciousness sort of grows up around it.

Talking about it is the best thing. The tendency is that women want to talk, but men don't and that can be a difficulty. Men tend to grieve, or not grieve, in different ways. In our culture, you're just not supposed to talk about it if you are a man.

Referring back to our discussion that life is a series of narrative stories, even the death of a child is an important story that can contribute to greater love. The death of a child is a big part of anybody's story. People come in to our lives and sometimes leave in what seem to be untimely exits. But I think there is a broader perspective, that all these things weave together.

We have two younger children who were adopted at birth and, oh my God, what a wonderful experience. My wife and I don't take the kids to any religious ceremonies and we don't talk about life after death at home. That's my professional life. We talk about homework, what's for dinner, and what's on TV tonight. But both of them have related memories of specifically choosing to come to us. That has really focused me on this idea that we live not just one, but many lives.

6 WILL I SEE MY DEPARTED LOVED ONES AGAIN?

IF SO, HOW CAN I BEST COMMUNICATE WITH THEM NOW?

ANITA MOORJANI

Our loved ones are actually around us and guiding us all the time. It's actually a lot easier than you may think to communicate with them. I just get into a quiet room and speak to them as though they're there because they are. Spend some time by yourself and just call on whomever you want to speak to whether it's a departed spouse or partner, child, or parent. When we communicate with our departed loved ones, we don't need to actually speak full sentences. You can just think about them and they will know what you want them to know. You don't have to worry about your thoughts being nasty or that you'll be judged or condemned. Don't worry at all because your departed loved ones love you unconditionally.

My father and I had a very turbulent relationship before he passed on ten years before my NDE. When I was in the other realm, I met my father; he was without his physical body and so was I. I realized that when our physical body goes, we also lose our gender, race, religion, beliefs, and all those filters that have accumulated over a lifetime. All that was left was pure consciousness, *pure essence*. His essence and my essence merged.

Now, I have the most beautiful relationship with my father because I'm encountering his pure essence that is nothing but unconditional love. So even if you had a bad relationship with someone who passed away, don't worry about it. Don't hold on to any negative feelings. They want you to be happy and and find your joy. They want you to free yourself from any negative emotions because they are free from them. When we're in physical life, we react to each other through all our layers of filters. When we die, we lose all of that. So you can communicate with departed loved ones freely and know they are not holding onto any baggage.

Finally, if your spouse or partner has died, he or she will not feel jealous if you meet someone else. In fact, nothing will make them happier than for you to be happy again. They know that life is a precious gift; we in the physical realm need to know that too and make the most of every single day.

P.M.H. ATWATER

Most people, not everyone, but most people see their loved ones, people and animals, when they pass over. How can you contact them now? It's very common and natural to receive communications from your loved ones after they die. You can learn to do this through prayer, meditation, visualization, or journaling. Just feel your love for them and know that whatever you sense is probably your departed loved one responding.

Talk to them. You can talk to them out loud. Dreams are another incredible way that many people use to get that contact. Sometimes the communication won't come to you, but will come through another person. For example, your neighbor will get a communication from your brother who died. I don't know why it happens that way but it happens a lot.

MARK PITSTICK

There's no such thing as death so of course you do. Many near-death experiencers have told about glorious reunions when they clinically died. They saw their departed loved ones and even beloved pets that had died. After-death contacts are very common. Authentic mediums have communication accurate messages from deceased loved ones to many people. Connections with departed loved ones have been repeatedly demonstrated with electronic voice phenomena.

So you can be sure that there is a lovely reunion waiting for you when you do cross over. And you don't have to wait until you die to enjoy interacting with your departed loved ones in a continuing although different relationship.

Over 75 million Americans have experienced *after-death contacts* or ADCs. The breakdown is 25 to 33 percent of the general population, 66 percent of widows and widowers, and 75 percent of parents whose children have passed on. These are incredible numbers and some of them are documented. So it's clear that at least some ADCs are not just the result of wishful thinking or imagination.

Evidential ADCs involve experiences in which information is conveyed that could not have been learned unless, indeed, there was communication with a departed spirit. Drs. Elizabeth Kubler-Ross, Carl Jung, Raymond Moody and others have reported these. It's clear that ADCs are on the up-and-up so, when a departed loved one passes on, keep your senses alert. Don't automatically cast off oddities such as objects being moved as, "That must have just been my imagination" or "I must have been daydreaming." Also, pay attention to unusual functioning of electronic devices since tampering with electronics seems to be easier for some in non-physical realms.

Once people learn about ADCs, they often ask, "Why haven't my departed loved ones contacted me?" I recently gave a workshop and a woman asked, "Why hasn't my father contacted me after he died two years ago?" It's an understandable question.

First of all, it's apparently not an easy feat to communicate from one dimension to another. Can you contact those in other realms? I can't, at least not at the time of this writing. So don't take the lack of contact personally. Your loved ones may be trying, but haven't yet mastered the technique. To get a better sense of this, watch the movie *Ghost* and how difficult it was for Patrick Swayze's character to manipulate a penny.

Next, soul time is different from earth time. Let's say that your loved one passed on two years ago; that may seem like only five minutes in spirit world. They may just be getting their bearings after completing healing showers, counseling, and re-orientation. They may be settling into the realization that time is a human construct and life is really all happening right now. So you might want to excuse them if they aren't contacting you *when* you want.

Also, consider that your loved ones in spirit world may have contacted you, but you didn't pick it up. You may want them to appear as you remember them and give you a big hug like they did while on earth. But this is a new moment so it's good to be flexible and open to them contacting you how they can.

Just recently, I counseled a couple whose only child died tragically. I felt his presence during the session and the next few days. While assembling this book, I was listening to the guests' recorded interviews and checking for accuracy against the typed transcripts. Everything was working fine and I got up to get a drink of water. When I came back, I could barely hear the audio. I checked everything I could think of with no results. Then I looked at the volume control at the top of my ITunes controls. The volume level had been turned all the way down. To do that requires clicking on an indicator and dragging it to the left. I didn't do it. Perhaps that was the little ones way of saying, "Hello. Thank you. Please tell my parents that I'm alive and well."

A final reason why you may not perceive visits from the Other Side is because you are not optimally receptive. You may need to be more on the same wavelength as your beloved deceased one. It's very similar to tuning into a certain radio frequency to listen to that station. In nonphysical realms, the energy is usually more peaceful and harmonious. If your energy is too sad or anxious, you may not be able to communicate.

That's why many after-death contacts occur during dreams. Your mind is quiet and relaxed; this enhances contact with those whose energies are higher and finer. And there are *validated dream ADCs* that show those are, at least sometimes, more than a dream.

The biggest key to having successful contacts with your departed loved ones is to remember that no one really dies. They really are alive and well so you don't have to worry about that. Your departed loved ones aren't a zillion trillion miles up in the sky somewhere. They may be in the same space as you right now. Even if you can't detect them with your five senses, you can with your heart and more ethereal senses.

MARILYN SCHLITZ

Perceiving departed loved ones can take different forms. There is the dreaming state. Some people say they never dream but we know they do, it's just that they're not remembering it. So it's helpful to learn to recall our dreams by setting an intention before we go to sleep at night. Keep a notepad near your bed and see what images come up.

Dr. Peter Fenwick, one of the people I've worked with and interviewed for my film, collected thousands of cases of people who, as they were dying, reported being visited by their loved ones. His findings suggest that these spirits were available to help make the death transition a smooth one. That's a comforting thought. As people begin to become familiar with this, they can invite in those guardians to help them. That becomes a means of connection.

People describe going to mediums and having some kind of communion with departed ones. That works for some people and not for others. For myself, I think you spend time in nature and be quiet. Spirit speaks through the trees, birds and animals; that can become a way of feeling connected to life and to the departed. All this assists a sense of a seamlessness between what is on this side and what potentially exists on the other.

GARY SCHWARTZ

I can speak as an authority having done so much research in this area. The evidence is clear. Absolutely, yes. When you die, you can reconnect with the people you love and who love you. Love is what connects us. And, when a child, parent, or loved one passes on, you can connect with that individual now. You can do that through mediums and can also develop that capacity yourself by learning a new skill.

I can teach anyone to play chopsticks on the piano, but very few of us are going to become a concert pianist. If we want to become concert pianists, we have to put the time and energy in and practice. The same thing applies to the skill of being able to connect with the other side.

In the future, I think it's going to be just like you and I talking over a great expanse. You're in Ohio, I'm in Arizona; I can't see you and you can't see me. But I'm talking over a wireless phone via a satellite that sends signals back down to you. We take that technology for granted and I foresee, sooner than later, that we'll have the technology to connect with the other side as well.

Communication with departed loved ones can seem more subtle that most people expect and that's why they might dismiss it. Let's get back to looking up at the sky at night where we can see thousands of stars with the naked eye. But during the day, we look up at the sky and see no stars. The question is what happened to all the starlight of thousands of stars we can see at night?

Did all that starlight disappear or it is still there and we just can't see it because we're blinded by the brightness of the sun? Sometimes we need to go into the dark in order to see the light. This information is subtle, it's below the level of our usual conscious experience. That's why people went to caves. That's why people learn to meditate. That's why mediums still their minds and get their emotions out of the way, so they can pick up the subtle cues that are really there.

CAROLINE MYSS

I have to base my answer on near-death experiences. There are two parallel realities going on. One is reincarnation. Can you still know your departed loved one if the soul has already reincarnated? On the other hand, if there's no such thing as time since that's a factor of the physical world, then all lives are simultaneous. We have no way of comprehending what simultaneous lives are or how that works. So I think we should trust that there is a cosmic structure in place that is probably very benevolent and we will encounter souls that we travel together with again.

BILL GUGGENHEIM

Yes, we will have contact with our deceased loved ones who are awaiting us. They know when we're going to arrive and they'll meet us when we cross over after our body dies. We'll continue on in what are known as soul groups and enjoy other lives with them in different roles. I may be someone's son in this life, but the mother, father, brother or sister in another life here on earth. And who knows what other roles may exist in other lifetimes in different forms on other planets?

Can they communicate with us now? That's what our book *Hello from Heaven* is all about. We interviewed two thousand people and collected 3300 accounts of people who had been contacted by a loved one who had died. In the United States, at least one hundred million people or one-third of our population have had contact with a family member or a friend who has died. This is direct and spontaneous contact without any mediums, psychics, or devices involved.

For people who haven't had an after-death communication yet, there are things they can do to enhance that. The easiest and simplest way is to learn how to meditate. Some people associate mediation with Eastern spiritual practices, but it's now more widely accepted in the West. Meditation is nothing more than learning how to relax deeply. Those who have done it become more open intuitively; I call these intuitive spiritual experiences. By opening our intuitive senses of feeling, seeing, smelling and touching, we can be contacted by our loved ones who have died.

I picture them as standing at our doorway, knocking, waiting for us to sense their presence, to feel that they're nearby, and hear their voices. But we're so busy and so limited by living in this physical world of our five senses. Even if we begin to have an ADC experience, we may abort it because doesn't fit in with what we believe is real. We're limited by religious teachings and an overemphasis on materialism. Science and technology, that's what many people believe in the most. But science does not accept anything beyond what it can measure with instruments and that can be difficult with things like afterlife.

Our departed loved ones want to communicate and, what we found over and over in our research, they want us to know they're okay. We don't have to worry about them. They're fine—they're much more fine than we are. They're in perfect health and everything is beautiful, fantastic. They want to come back and let us know they still exist and that they'll meet us when we make our own transition. Most of all, they want us to know that they love us, they value us, and they look forward to being with us again.

BERNIE SIEGEL

I can only speak from my experiences of hearing voices. It's like somebody is talking to me while I'm out taking a walk, jogging, riding a bike. A voice will speak to me and when that voice speaks, I listen. To give you a brief example, the day my father was going to die, I was out exercising before I went to the hospital and a voice said, "How did your parents meet?" I said, "I don't know." And the voice said "Ask your mother when you get to the hospital." I walked into the hospital room and what pops out of me? It's almost like that voice, not me, because I didn't say anything compassionate, didn't hug anyone, I just asked, "How did you two meet?"

My mother started telling stories because of that question and they were all very funny. My father lost a coin toss and had to take her out on the first date. She started with that and it got worse from there. My father died laughing, looking wonderful, and everybody in the room was in a sense stunned by the experience.

My mother died a few years later and I got a call from Monica, a psychic who didn't know my parents. She said, "Your folks are together again. They are proud of you and are being shown around by someone who likes chocolate and cigarettes. Oh, Elizabeth Kubler-Ross is showing your folks around." Monica didn't know that Elizabeth was a really good friend of mine who helped me in my journey.

I always talk about finding pennies as a sign from God. This is a message: liberty, in God we trust, and Abe Lincoln who reminds us of our physical mortality. After my mother died, I found close to three dozen pennies. We have a long driveway and I would go down to our mailbox. On the way back, I would see pennies on the driveway. I would not have missed them on the way down, so how did they get there?

I think there are several reasons why people may not detect visits from their departed loved ones. People could be thinking too much. It helps to what I call "take the lid off." It's like opening up your consciousness. Years ago, I was having difficulties with my father's death and the whole concept of death and he appeared to me in a dream looking wonderful with a big smile. That took care of it for me. Visualize the people who died so they know it's okay for them to come back, that they are not going to hurt or upset you.

Don't look for your deceased loved ones necessarily, but look for signs, things that interested them. A son died as a teenager; he had a collection of butterflies in his room and was studying them all the time. The father went for a walk in Connecticut and a beautiful butterfly came to him and followed him. The father went home and looked it up in his son's room. It was a butterfly that lives only in South America. How did it get to Connecticut?

A woman was talking about her murdered daughter who loved birds. They had an outdoor wedding for her sister and a bird interrupted the wedding. Everybody said, "It's your daughter." Later, a bird flew in through an open window and, of course, everyone's reaction was, "It's your daughter." I could go on and on with these stories, especiallyfrom parents of children who die.

When you are in a room with other parents and the door gets shut, they are not afraid to tell stories.

So keep your mind open and look for these signs. Don't think, worry, or be too intellectual about it. Just let it happen in your sleep or meditation.

STAN GROF

A very common observation in thanatology is people who are in the process of dying have a vision of what has been called *the welcoming committee*, people who died before them. Their friends and relatives appear and communicate with the dying person about the realm beyond. Dr. Moody created a psychomanteum with special conditions where the incidence of these experiences was greatly enhanced. In ancient Greece, people were inspired by visits underground and looking into a large copper kettle full of water with a special kind of illumination. They experienced visits from departed loved ones in a significant number of cases and Dr. Moody was able to replicate that.

In my book *When the Impossible Happens,* I report instances where people actually encountered their deceased relatives in what I call the holotropic state of consciousness. This was more than just having a vision of these relatives. The people had, of course, known them before they died and it would be easy to visually reconstruct these images. I described several instances where the circumstances were such that we could confirm it was more than just a vision.

For example, my colleague Dr. Walter Pahnke disappeared in the Atlantic while diving and his body was never found, the equipment was never found. His wife Eva had great problems accepting his death because he was so full of energy, went for a dive, and then she didn't see him anymore. She had a psychedelic session and I was the sitter. During the session, Walter appeared and had a long communication with her and then the session was interrupted because she had to go to the bathroom. She told me about it and said, "This cannot be true. Is this some kind of a wishful feeling fantasy of mine?"

When she returned to the session, Walter appeared again and said, "I want to ask you a favor. Would you return a book that I borrowed from a friend of mine?" He gave the exact description of where to find it, which room and shelf. Eva didn't have any knowledge of this. As soon as the session was over, we followed his instructions and there was the book. I have a couple of other examples in the book and many others in my records.

We can perceive our departed loved ones in different ways. Sometimes there's a vision of the person, sometimes it's more a sensing of their presence and a telepathic communication.

KAREN WYATT

Yes, we will see our departed loved ones again, but it may be different than we are used to. For example, my mother passed away two years ago and she left her physical body and earthly identity behind. When I die and my soul merges back into the spiritual realm, I will be able to reconnect with my mother's soul. But she will not be the same person that I knew here on Earth and neither will I. We will both be our pure soul essences when we reconnect in that realm.

However, while I'm still here on this planet, her soul can reconnect with me through that physical and personality identity that I knew before. If I desire it, her soul can reconnect with me and we can communicate.

It is my firm belief that God exists, heaven exists, and our souls are immortal living spirits. We can communicate with those souls now and, after we die, we will be reunited with our loved ones in the Light. I base that belief on my own faith, experience, and the science of near-death experiences and survival of consciousness studies.

In my work as a psychic medium, I have had many spirits tell me who greeted them when they crossed into the Light. And the client who I am reading for is just flabbergasted at how I could know about the friends and relatives who have come forward. In near-death experience studies, when a person crosses into the Light, they come into contact with people who have died, not those who are alive.

There was an interesting case study in Japan where a woman died on the operating table but was resuscitated. Afterwards, she said, "It was so odd because I saw my sister on the Other Side, but she's not dead." Her parents said, "Well, you didn't know this, but she was killed in a car accident yesterday." So, she did not know her sister had passed, yet she encountered her sister's spirit on the other side. So there's science to back this up, experiences that myself and other mediums have had, and teachings of great spiritual leaders who tell us there is a better world to come.

People can absolutely communicate with their departed loved ones now through a medium or after-death contacts while awake or dreaming. Many people report a departed loved one visiting in a dream, but it wasn't really a dream, it was a realistic conversation. There's a difference between a dream and a visitation.

While awake, people report catching a glimpse of a loved one out of their peripheral vision or suddenly smelling a familiar scent associated with a person although there is no source for that. They may turn on the radio while driving and there's that song that makes them think of that person. Objects can move, for example, they come home to find a photo album on the table that just happens to be open to a picture of the person who died. There are all types of contact experiences.

Spirits reach out from the Other Side to let us know they're alive and well. The issue is whether or not people are open to these contacts, if they are aware of them, and willing to accept them as reality. Our loved ones are around us and reach out to make contact.

In my book *Never Letting Go* is a chapter called *How Spirits Contact Us* that discusses several ways they do this. Let's say you're driving in your car and you're thinking about your son who died. Then you turn on the radio and there's a song by Maroon 5 that he used to listen to all the time. Is that just a coincidence? Spirits are pure energy and communicate to us through waves or frequencies. They cannot only hear our thoughts, they are also aware of radio waves. So what spirits do is direct your attention and prompt you to turn the radio on at the right moment.

Other people say, "Every time we talk about our deceased mom, the lights in this room flicker." People might say that's really farfetched, but why does it happen to so many people worldwide? It's because spirits reach out to us and they're using impulses of electricity. Spirits are beings of energy and can interfere with electrical fields.

A client may say, "My husband hasn't visited me since he died. But I do have these dreams where he speaks to me." I then ask the client, "Do the dreams seem real?" "Oh yes, they don't seem like dreams at all, they seem like actual conversations."

That's because when we go into the sleep state, the brain wave pattern goes from the waking beta state into alpha as we drift into sleep. As we go into deeper sleep, we go into theta levels. During the alpha and theta levels, brainwave frequencies become slower so there's less anxiety and over-analysis. Spirits can detect that, align their brainwave frequencies with yours, and get a frequency match.

It's just like tuning into a radio station: we're at 89.5, they're at 101.7 so you meet somewhere around 99.3. That's the theory about how spirit communication works. So you can have the experience and accept and rejoice in it. Or you can crossexamine it: "Oh, that couldn't be true, it's just my imagination, this is impossible." And there's nothing wrong with doing that— it's a very human thing, especially for males. Women tend to be more accepting of these experiences because spirit communications are an emotionally-based activity and women tend to handle their emotions better than men. So the choice is yours whether or not you want to give yourself permission to have this experience and to accept that it's real. *(Mark Anthony, the Psychic Lawyer, author of Never Letting Go and Evidence of Eternity)*

RAYMOND MOODY

Many people have experienced what they believed were contacts with their departed loved ones. I don't know why some have contacts and some don't.

There is an ancient modality that's known all over the world for evoking perceptions of the deceased by gazing into clear depths. This was done in Japan with little ponds of water and arched bridges over them. In Greece, people went underground and gazed into a mirrored cauldron. You also can discern departed loved ones by gazing into mirrors. This was a well-known custom in the United States until the early twentieth century when people began to listen more to radio and then TV.

There's also an ancient method of dream incubation. You write a letter to a person who has died, ask questions, and talk about your feelings. Then you fold the letter, put it under your mattress, and forget about it. In many cases, this will bring about a sort of nighttime vision that may or may not be experienced as a dream that seems more real than usual.

From my experience, I wouldn't attach any particular significance to not receiving a contact from your departed loved ones. Don't assume that there is some kind of rift there or some problem because we just can't understand all the circumstances we're dealing with. The afterlife is like another dimension of reality that is arched over this one. There's a structure in mathematics called the Poincare Disc, the intersection of Euclidean and hyperbolic planes. It shows there can be structures that are infinite from within, but finite from without. I think that we on Earth are within one of those.

7

ARE THERE GHOSTS AND EVIL SPIRITS?

AND, IF SO, WHAT ARE THEY?

ANITA MOORJANI

I don't believe that anyone is truly evil. I think it's our own fears here on earth that can misinterpret things and believe it's evil. The spirit of someone can linger if loved ones on earth are excessively attached. But once someone crosses over, I don't believe there is really such a thing as an evil spirit. There are a lot of people who have been conditioned to believe in evil and their minds interpret accordingly. Unexplainable events may seem like ghost activity, but the underlying cause isn't evil. It may just be our deceased loved ones who want to attract our attention.

P.M.H. ATWATER

Before my near-death experiences, I did a research project about psychic phenomena and was a ghost buster. What I've found and seen is that sometimes there are troubled spirits. When some people die, they don't go on into the Light. They hang around in a netherworld because of a strong promise that they would stay. Or they could be lost; they just don't know what to do next after they die. Others are still caught up in evil so they stick around after dying. A person may die cursing someone and wants to stick around because he is still infused with anger and wants to get even.

There is possession, there are mixed-up spirits doing not so nice things. That's why I caution people who get into the Ouija board, channeling, mediums, or whatever. If they don't know what they're doing, it's very helpful to get training to understand what is the voice of evil or confusion versus the voice of God

You can protect yourself from ghosts or evil spirits. You can do that through prayer, meditation, taking care of yourself, and understanding your own emotions and thoughts.

MARK PITSTICK

Some statistics about the subject are that 20% of Americans believe they have experienced a ghost contact while 50% believe in ghosts. There are university studies, for example at UCLA and Cambridge, well-done scientific studies that show something is going on. The research primarily records aberrations of light in videos or photographs as shown, for example, in the respected magazine *Popular Photography.* So some research is there to show that, yes, there appear to be what we call ghosts or stuck spirits.

In most near-death experiences, clinically dead people see the Light and go into it, but they are not forced to do so. It's a matter of choice. It appears that the souls of ghosts don't enter the Light after dying. These unfortunate ones are in a sort of purgatory or netherworld between earth and the next phase of life. This can occur for several reasons:

1. While on earth, they were atheists with absolutely no spiritual or religious beliefs. After dying, there is a temporary carry-over of earth-formed beliefs. After their body dies, their minds still believe there's nothing, so that's their experience—at least initially. Forever is a long time, however, and eventually they are very likely to notice they are still conscious and agree with Descarte's proposition, "I think, therefore I am."

2. They were agnostics and seriously doubted whether there is an afterlife so the pattern is the same as #1. (By the way, I've found that many atheists and agnostics are understandably reacting to ridiculous images of a big guy in the sky who arbitrarily judges, smites, and burns forever. More sensible images may appeal to them, a Force or Intelligence that creates and sustains all life.)

3. They had a violent or sudden death and were in shock when they passed on. They may have not seen the Light or decided not to enter it. The stronger a person's spiritual foundation during the earth-experience, the more she is prepared for such occurrences, thus religious advice to build your house (life) on granite, not shifting sand.

4. The recently departed soul had strong negative emotions such as jealousy, guilt, or anger. They may not want to enter the Light because they seek revenge or some other perceived solution to their negative emotions. For these reasons, they were not ready to move on to the next realm, but that can change whenever they are ready.

5. They had addictions to excessive food, materialism, sex, alcohol, drugs, sports, etc. Some mediums have observed stuck spirits hovering around intoxicated bar patrons. These ghosts may be trying to get a contact high and vicariously experience alcohol because they can't obtain it in nonphysical realms.

Some people ask, "Can a ghost hurt me?" From my perspective, the answer is no, they can't hurt you. But they can scare you a lot: your hair may stand on end, you may get cold chills, run into a wall, or fall down stairs. However, that's not the ghost hurting you—that's you hurting or scaring yourself. While on earth, it's wise to protect yourself; likewise be cautious and shield yourself when interacting with stuck spirits.

People wonder about the difference between ghost visitations versus departed loved ones visiting during an after-death contact. There's usually a clear difference. Ghost visits often engender feelings of darkness, cold, fear, and hopelessness. Sensitive persons, especially, can feel the negative energies that can occur when entities are in limbo.

After-death contacts, on the other hand, are characterized by feelings of peace, love, and reassurance that your departed loved one is alive and well. ADCs leave you feeling comforted and hopeful that life does indeed continue after physical death. They feel more confident that they will see their departed loved ones again because they just had a meaningful visit.

On occasion, however, the difference isn't always so obvious. One woman told me that her house seemed haunted for several months: it felt cold, there were sounds of stomping on the stairs, and she couldn't sleep. Then she realized it was probably her son-in-law who had died suddenly and tragically and was trying to get her attention. She spoke aloud, telling him she would find someone to help him move into the Light and, immediately, the room felt warmer and looked brighter.

She found a medium who assisted his transition into the next phase of life and the "hauntings" ended. So, there's a case where an apparent ghost visit was really a departed loved one trying to communicate in the best way he could given his lower, denser energies at the time.

Praying for stuck entities and encouraging them to enter the Light is sometimes a sufficient solution. If not, you might want to call in someone who has experience and skill—a so-called *ghostbuster* in the form of a medium, shaman, or energy worker. And if that doesn't work, I'm pretty sure Dan Aykroyd and Bill Murray are still doing some of that work on the side.

Regarding evil, the Aramaic meanings for evil and devil meant 'wild and chaotic energy.' Just as on Earth, some souls are imbalanced. They are weak and confused—much like cancer cells and can impact vulnerable people. Their actions might be reprehensible, but that doesn't mean they're evil. There's a difference between the doer and the deed.

I do not believe in a personified powerful evil being like the devil although the pitchfork, red skin, and horns is really imaginative. Why would the loving intelligence Source and Sustainer of all life create such an opposing being? And what loving parents would allow any powerful evil being to hurt their children?

My best advice is not even dwell on evil. Surround yourself with prayers each day and align yourself with good and God. Love yourself and stay aligned with the Source and your spiritual support team. Darkness and evil have no real power over light and love. As with all matters, focus on what you want, not what you don't want.

MARILYN SCHLITZ

There are people who have fears about ghosts and evil spirits and some religious traditions have cultivated those fears. Several people I've interviewed were raised in very fundamentalist upbringings where there was a lot of talk about hell and damnation. That's scary to think that's what you're heading into, but those beliefs are only held by certain groups. It's helpful if people can liberate themselves from these kinds of inhibiting worldviews and begin to see other possibilities.

In some traditions it is believed that spirits can be mischievous and seem to create harm. The Day of the Dead celebrations are held—in part—to appease the spirits, to keep them happy, and let them know they're respected and still part of the family.

This topic can be another opportunity for us to reflect on our own worldviews. Ultimately, it invites each of us to consider what seems most true.

GARY SCHWARTZ

Well, that's probably the most controversial and taboo topic in all of science if not all of humanity. Many years ago, I started thinking about the physics of consciousness and survival of consciousness. It became very clear to me that what allows your and my consciousness, energy, information, to continue after it dies is the same for any living system after it dies.

The consciousness of the Hitlers and Bin Ladens of the world continues on just as much as the consciousness of the Mother Theresas and Martin Luther Kings. Energy is energy, information is information. Individuals don't automatically lose their malevolent tendencies because they die; there's not instant enlightenment. Consequently, the negativity continues. Once you recognize this, then you say, "Wow, then I have to be protected from this."

What kind of protection is literally built in the structure of the cosmos? My working hypothesis is that a "veil" exists as protection from the Source so we will not be potentially harmed by "negative forces" that continue to exist.

For the record, science doesn't want to touch this with a hundred and ten foot pole. The implication is that all consciousness survives because all energy survives. The notion that so-called evil or dark forces, both individual and collective, survive has to be entertained. Science does not want to address these questions and the public is frightened about this.

It is wise for us to be frightened about this, but that doesn't mean we have to be terrified by it. There are different ways to minimize the impact of negative forces and protect ourselves. We can develop *spiritual immunity*, just as we have biological immunity, by using spiritual practices such as connecting with God, living in love, and so on. All of that appears to really work.

CAROLINE MYSS

Yes, ghosts exist. I have quite frequently been in places where I have sensed the presence of restless spirits. Do people who have passed on stay here for whatever reason? I would say yes. I've actually seen one, but I have felt others. And why do they stay here? I'm not sure about that. I've heard speculations such as they died suddenly.

What I will say is that in all spiritual traditions, there is a sacrament, a teaching, a ritual to help a spirit collect all of its soul fragments before it passes over. What that suggests is that we can die consciously with a sense of, "I have finished what I came here to do." That means if we don't die consciously, there must be a consequence.

It's a bad thing if someone is a thief or has a bad temper. But what's unforgivable or really carries bad karma is murder. When you kill a human

---

being, you tamper with their life path and that, in turn, tampers with the life paths of countless other souls. It affects those who were supposed to meet that person. There's a whole network of threads. And so to that extent, is the person who was murdered a ghost because they didn't finish something?

What is an evil spirit? Well, that opens the question, is there evil? And the answer is yes. Is an evil spirit a demon? Yes. I acknowledge the whole world of demons because you can't have angels and not have demons; they're partners. So yes, there are evil spirits.

BILL GUGGENHEIM

Our research did not include ghosts or evil spirits. I think they are beings with low consciousness. There are certainly many people in our world who commit unspeakable crimes shooting children in schools, bombing people at the Boston Marathon, and on and on. You don't have to be concerned about evil on the other side. There are plenty of people with evil intentions are this side of life. Too many.

Someone told us a story that we didn't use in our book for obvious reasons. Ted Bundy killed many young women and was executed in prison. After his death, one woman wanted to contact his soul. She went into a meditative state and kept trying to call him toward her. As she did, she described a mountain of black slime moving slowly toward her. She became scared and woke herself up to end the experience. I think that's what, symbolically at least, Bundy's consciousness could be like. So you want to be careful that you don't attract evil to you and don't become influenced by that. It's rare. You have to seek it out. They're not trying to contact us, nor can they unless we provide an opening for that.

BERNIE SIEGEL

It depends on your definition of a ghost. I'd say they are a manifestation of consciousness. I got an email about two people in a family who had been killed in an accident and a member of the family had a wedding soon after that. They didn't postpone the wedding and had those disposable cameras for everybody. When the pictures were developed, there were clouds shaped like people around tables of the families of the two people who had died. That was a mystical experience for everybody.

Do I think there are spirits? I have to say there are because of what people have said to me and what they have seen. Carl Jung said the future is unconsciously prepared long in advance therefore can be glimpsed by clairvoyants. I think these gifted people can quiet their minds and communicate with departed spirits. I do believe we have spirits around us whether you call it energy, consciousness or something else. I don't let belief limit my life. If I experience something, I believe it even if I can't explain it or understand how it happens. But I know it happens.

STAN GROF

The Swiss psychiatrist Carl Gustav Jung had some powerful experiences of this. At one point in his life, he was going through what we call a spiritual emergency where there was such an influx from his deep unconscious. He felt the presence of many spirits and other members of his family experienced them as well. He channeled and wrote one of his most remarkable texts, The Seven Sermons to the Dead.

We have a very narrow image of the psyche and what I call the cartography of the psyche. Dr. Jung vastly expanded this and talked about the collective unconscious. So what we call ghosts, in my opinion, could just be visions, images that come from this collective unconscious. There are many other

---

important experiences, for example, images of deities from different cultures, demonic entities, visits to the beyond, paradises, heavens, and so on. Visions of ghosts could be just one unusual category of experiences that we can have.

Again, we ask the questions, "Are these real? Do they have what we would call ontological reality?" Dr. Rupert Sheldrake, the revolutionary English biologist, spent some time investigating and describing this, for example, with haunted houses. We are not just talking about individual experiences, but something that has been experienced simultaneously by a number of people. Certain castles have the reputation of being haunted and people who visit repeatedly report these experiences. Many of these discarnate apparitions that we call ghosts actually have the form of deceased people.

KAREN WYATT

I think that there are immature, wounded, or damaged souls that may have difficulty merging back into the spiritual realm after the time of death. Their energy may stay in the Earth plane so we might be aware of them. They are minimally harmful. I think they are lost, confused, and may not have had the opportunity to find their way back to the spiritual realm where they belong.

These lost souls might need some healing from us. They also might need more experience on planet earth and that's another reason why they remain here. They may need to learn something about life on Earth that they didn't pick up while they were incarnated on the planet.

MARK ANTHONY

Many people want there to be evil spirits, demons and devils. I'm not a big believer in negative energy, although jerks die every minute. When someone negative and evil like Osama bin Laden or Adolph Hitler dies, they cross to the

Other Side. Their egos remain behind and they have to reflect on what they've done, but they're certainly not evil spirits. I also don't believe in hell or the devil. It's ridiculous to think that God created a negative entity to fight with for all of eternity but then, like a Viking hero, prevails at the very end. Once again, this is all Bronze Age superstition from the past.

However, there are different frequencies on the Other Side. The higher frequencies would be what I call the heavenly dimensions whereas the lower frequencies are more removed from God. There is also a multitude of intelligent, non-human, spiritual entities. Some are more aligned with plant, earth, or animal life. They're not negative or evil, they are just operating on a different radio frequency, so to speak.

There are three theories about ghosts and hauntings. Let's take a quick look at them...

1. *A spirit is trapped here on Earth.* I don't believe that, even though in Never Letting Go, I talk about spirits who linger in a place for a while. The Other Side is without time, it's timeless, so spirits may be in a location for what we think of as twenty, thirty, or forty years. However, on the Other Side, it seems like just a few moments. Spirit beings are also aware that they have the ability to let go of this world and transition into the Light anytime.

2. *It's a spirit that travels between Earth and the Other Side to visit.* Do souls come back and forth? Yes they do, all the time. But that doesn't mean they are ghosts. It can be quite unnerving when a spirit communicates with you because they're pure energy. That energy interfaces with your electrical field and the physiological response can be hairs standing on end or cold chills. Therefore, we think it must be negative when it really isn't.

3. *It's not a spirit at all, but a residual energy echo.* Matter retains energy. Let's say a murder or other tragedy happens in a location. The energy is like an echo, and the echo continues. This particular type of "ghost" is no more an immortal living spirit than your reflection in a mirror is a living person. It's a reflection or an echo that keeps getting replayed and replayed. You can pick up on it and it feels like a spiritual entity. These residual energy echoes can be interrupted and stopped, for example, by a house clearing and getting the negative energy out. But it is not a spirit. *(Mark Anthony, the Psychic Lawyer, author of Never Letting Go and Evidence of Eternity)*

8 WHAT HAPPENS TO THE SOUL/LIFE-FORCE OF PEOPLE WHO COMMIT SUICIDE?

ANITA MOORJANI

When people commit suicide, they usually do so as a last resort after a lot of suffering and feeling very lost and lonely. When they cross over, they receive pure love, compassion and empathy. There's no judgment. I want to assure others that your loved one who committed suicide is absolutely not getting punished or judged. He or she is not going to get any bad karma or be forced to do it all over again. I also want loved ones of a suicide to know it's not their fault. A lot of people feel guilty that they didn't see the signs or they weren't there for their loved ones. It is absolutely not your fault. Sometimes, it happens no matter how much you are there. Some people feel very alone no matter how much they are surrounded by others. You can still speak to your deceased loved ones who killed themselves and they still love you unconditionally. They do not blame you for what happened.

P.M.H. ATWATER

We confront this head-on in near-death research. The majority of people who attempt suicide but come back have a very positive experience on the Other Side. They return with a resolve to use that experience to turn their lives around here and make their lives better. However, there are some people who come back and are still very angry and go on to lead miserable lives.

I can't say that suicide is wrong for everybody because that's a very big statement to make and the evidence does not support that. I can say that the vast majority of near-death experiencers come back feeling that life on earth is worth it and purposeful. Yes, they would like to go back to the Light, but they don't try suicide again. They feel there's something they need to accomplish on this side and, until they do, they will not be able to go back.

There are some near-death experiencers, especially children, who do try suicide again. But most of them conclude they better stay here in their body because this is where they can start, this is where the opportunities are, and it's better to stay.

MARK PITSTICK

This is a tough one. I did suicide prevention counseling and education in my twenties. I briefly thought about suicide when my first love broke up with me. I worked in hospitals and was with a number of people who died as a result of suicide. I've also helped those who attempted to die, but didn't. I've worked with families and friends whose loved ones took their own lives. So I've been around every phase of this issue and know it's tough for everyone involved.

But it's not an unforgivable sin, nor is there any such thing. And it's certainly not a one-way ticket to hell, nor is there any such place.

My comments about the spiritual impact of suicide come from my personal beliefs as well as input from authentic mediums, after-death contacts, spiritual regressions, near-death experiences, enlightened religious/spiritual views, and common sense.

A wide-range of after-life experiences can occur when a person commits suicide. It's not that different from the spectrum of possibilities when people die by any means. An elderly couple from New York both committed suicide years ago. He was in severe pain and was losing his physical capabilities. This minister couldn't take care of his wife who was losing her mind. They saw what their futures were going to be like and didn't want to end them in a nursing home. So they decided to take their lives in a way and timing of their choosing.

When a person is suffering with severe and chronic physical or/and mental pain and imbalance, who can judge when enough is enough?

At some point, it's time to pass on. Who is the ultimate authority about how and when that happens? The church? The government? Society? I believe it's the individual.

In earlier times, people died in more timely ways because there weren't life-sustaining technologies available. In native cultures, the tribe couldn't survive with the severely ill or very elderly draining its resources. So the infirm were left out where weather or animals killed them. That might sound savage and uncaring to us now in the 21st century, but have you seen what passes for "living" in nursing homes and other long-term care facilities? These people usually succumb from pneumonia or other infection after extended time on a ventilator while lying comatose in the fetal state. I've been around lots of this and it's not natural or dignified—but it does create a lot of income for the disease care industry.

To look at another example, consider a person who commits suicide for impulsive reasons. Let's say a teenager's first love breaks up and it feels like the end of the world. She may kill herself over that whereas a more mature and balanced person wouldn't. If that young person had waited just a little while longer, she could have seen that life goes on after heartbreak.

Her impulsive actions don't mean she will go to hell forever since no such place exists. There's no judgment except for any temporary self-condemnation or regret. A soul in that situation may decide to come back into a similar scenario, but that's a choice. The next time around, perhaps she can rise to the occasion and master that challenge rather than committing suicide.

We live in a difficult time right now for maintaining mental health. Living in the 21st century has lots of advantages, but there are serious health concerns that impact the brain. Heavy metals and chemicals abound in our food, water, body care products, home cleaning products, and other sources. The brain is very sensitive to these stressors such as herbicides and pesticides. Nutritional deficiencies can also result in significant "mental" symptoms. Some people are like canaries in a coalmine who warn others that these toxins are making people mentally imbalanced.

We see this everyday in our holistic health care practice and use *Nutrition Response Testing* (NRT) to remove these stressors and address nutritional deficiencies that often cause depression, anxiety, panic attacks, etc. A healthfully raised, chemical-free, GMO-free diet, whole food supplements, and optimal self-care usually work wonders. Visit www.unsinc.info to find a NRT practitioner near you.

Another reason people are having so many mental symptoms is the excessive use of prescription drugs by the medical profession. Medical care is unparalleled in the U.S. for crisis and emergency care. However, people are often given too many harmful medications with potential side-effects such as increased suicidal and homicidal thinking or behavior. Of all the school shooters, most or all were on antidepressant medications.

For all the reasons above and others, I understand why a person may take his life. Certainly the Energy/Intelligence that created and sustains the cosmos understands as well.

Finally, the topic of assisted suicide is a big one, especially with the baby boomer population aging and dying. They are well-known for doing things their way and questioning authority. Would people handle *end-of-this-life* issues if they really knew they are infinite beings?

There should be other options for having euthanasia—*a good death*—rather than doing the long downhill suffering approach. That route makes a lot of money for big business, but doesn't best serve people's needs and is bankrupting our economy. We wouldn't let our pets suffer the way some humans do. We can do better than that and will as more people realize death is just another phase in never-ending life.

MARILYN SCHLITZ

It's a time when we think deeply since suicide certainly involves suffering and pain. It obviously touches all of us and we feel the grief of everyone in that person's life.

I advocate the right to choose how and when a person dies. There comes a time in a person's life, particularly under certain kinds of disease and conditions, where it becomes appropriate to choose a transition that alleviates their suffering. Our culture's huge denial of death has pathologized the process of dying. To the extent we can reinvigorate our awareness about death, we can help alleviate additional suffering when people are ready to make that transition.

My own spiritual view is that the state of mind we're in at the moment of our transition is going to be very important for what may come next. So whatever the method of passing is, we can hold clarity and a sense of peace. I don't know if that's what I'll achieve in the end, but it's certainly what I aspire to. I hope that people can make their transition with the most clarity, calmness, and purpose. A dear friend of mine, Dr. Willis Harmon, was near the end of his life and was really ready for the next great adventure; he is a great inspiration to me. What a great way of viewing death. If death is a change in our frequency, not necessarily the content but the frequency of our being, then it is important that we be able to make that transition smoothly.

GARY SCHWARTZ

Suicide is not suicide is not suicide. Some people commit suicide because they are severely grief stricken and depressed. After they pass on, the evidence suggests that they wake up and realize their actions had been affected by their tremendous challenges. A subset of that group will decide that they made a mistake and regret having taken their own lives and causing so much pain to others. There are various ways they can respond: by giving back to those who they love on Earth, caring for those on the Other Side, or returning to the Earth again.

Other people commit suicide because they feel they're no longer of service and can't help their family. They don't want to take up any more resources. In some Native American traditions, when people felt they were a burden on the tribe, they believed they would be of more service to become an ancestor. They would go out into the desert and die. This was also suicide, but they weren't doing it out of depression or anger—they were doing it out of love. They would continue to be members of the tribe, but from the ancestral rather than the physical realm.

I think that suicide is often tragic for the individual and loved ones, but it's also an opportunity for growth.

CAROLINE MYSS

I don't know. I think this is a loving, benevolent universe and when somebody is at the point of suicide, they're not rational, they're hurting, they're in so much pain that they're not making a conscious, clear act. I don't believe in Dante's eternal version of hell so I'll leave it at that.

BILL GUGGENHEIM

In a way it's sad that you're asking the question; I'm not blaming you because I used to ask the same question myself. I am a bereaved father and my forty-seven year old daughter took her own life with a handgun almost three years ago because of depression. She had gone off her medications, which she had quite a few of, after someone convinced her to do that cold turkey. She then had a time when she was more lucid and told her sister she might begin taking them again, but she didn't. Then I think she began falling down a black endless hole of depression. She bought a handgun and used it the same day and that was the end of her physical life.

The good part is I've not only heard from her several times since then, I've also seen her. I've had a series of ADC's with her. We have so many labels for people who take their own lives but this is just another form of death. You can die from an illness, accident, homicide or suicide. The books by Dr. Michael Newton make the point that we've all likely taken our own life numerous times. There's no penalty in the spiritual realms.

I'm not saying it's okay to kill yourself if you're feeling suicidal right now because you're going to hurt other people and there are better solutions. But those who do take their own lives are not treated any differently on the Other Side than those who die from other causes.

There's a beautiful book called *The Other Side of Suicide* by Karen Peebles that was dictated to her by her uncle who died by suicide. It shows that people who take their own lives are treated with a tremendous amount of love and acceptance on the Other Side because they need it. The souls of departed children often help out because they provide the most unconditional love of anyone. Some people who attempted to die by suicide had near-death experiences that were very positive. Others had painful, frightening experiences but if they called out for help, those immediately changed to positive ones.

There is a lot of mythology about suicide that's very false. It's more of a cultural or religious taboo than anything else. We look at the person who died by suicide differently and, perhaps more importantly, we treat their survivors differently. That's very unfortunate.

BERNIE SIEGEL

I say the same thing that happens to people who die of a disease, auto accident, or old age. They don't die. Their consciousness continues on and learns from its experiences.

I always say the biggest public health issue on the planet is parenting. There are studies done with college students that ask, "Did your parents love you?" If the answer was "no," 98 percent of them had suffered a major illness by middle-age but only 25 percent if the answer was "yes." The self-destruction comes because you don't feel like a child of God.

I know people who were told by parents: "You are a failure, you embarrass us. We didn't want you in the first place. You ought to commit suicide." And

I know parents who have committed suicide and said to their kids, "We don't love you enough to not kill ourselves." But my hope is that all these people learn something.

One young man I was helping had AIDS. He had been sexually abused. His parents… it was a horrible life. He called me because I was trying to help him survive and he said, "I'm going to commit suicide." I said, "Wait a minute, Tony. Instead of killing yourself, I can get you a guy who will kill your parents." He said, "No, I never want to be like them." His amazing statement touched my heart. I have to share the happy ending. When he went down to the subway station to jump in front of the A-train, it didn't show up so he called the suicide hotline. They rescued him and he said, "I learned about love from the people who came to help me."

In one study, 70 percent of high school students said they've contemplated suicide. What you need to do is eliminate what's killing you, not yourself. I don't mean kill your parents, but you can call the authorities and say, "My parents are abusing me. I need to get out of here." You can quit your job. You can end a marriage. Don't say, "I'll make this marriage work if it kills me." No, get out there because it's affecting your life and your health. Get the hell out of there, eliminate it. Don't kill yourself.

Whenever possible, be a love warrior. I know people with alcoholic parents who started saying "I love you" to them every morning. One woman returned to our support group with a big smile. I said what happened? She said, "For three months, nothing happened. Then, this morning I was late for work. I ran out of the house and my parents were yelling 'You forgot something.' I said 'What did I forget? I've got everything.' Her parents said, 'You forgot to say I love you.'" That's when they all started crying and hugging each other.

STAN GROF

Again, I have to report what I have heard from people that I have worked with. Their insights mostly focus on the idea that suicide is not a solution. It results in an unfinished karma; if we try to escape it, we are going to return to the same problems in the next incarnation. Whether this is some kind of ultimate truth is always an open question. Our observations would indicate that, yes, the consciousness of people who take their own lives continues on and has a chance to do it over again.

KAREN WYATT

Human beings have been given free will and we are able to use it during this lifetime. One of the possibilities of free will is that we can terminate our lives. A person may make a choice to do that if the lifetime is too difficult or just cannot be completed for some reason. Too much physical harm may have occurred or the soul may not be strong enough to carry the load. I don't believe there is punishment for anyone who chooses to end a lifetime.

After we die, there is a life review. I think some suicides could be by design and maybe by contract. An agreement might have been made before this lifetime and suicide would be a fulfillment of that contract. In other cases, suicide might be the result of being overwhelmed by a life that's too difficult or painful. In that case, the life review would allow that soul to look at what features of this lifetime made it so difficult to bear. That would help the soul choose experiences that might be more beneficial for the next incarnation. I don't believe there is any punishment, hell, or damnation for those who commit suicide. There is only love, compassion, and an opportunity to learn.

A lot of people contact me about loved ones who have committed suicide. In traditional Judaism, Christianity and Islam, those who commit suicide go to hell. And people are just devastated at the thought of a loved one burning forever. In my book *Evidence of Eternity,* I spend a lot of time discussing suicide. I can tell you this, there is no "one size fits all" to the question of what happens when they die.

The bottom line is we are all children of God, the most loving parent of all. No good earthly parents would ever condemn their child to an eternity of suffering. That doesn't mean there are not repercussions for our behaviors. But this Bronze Age sense of, you're being cast into the pit of fire forever... I don't mean to offend anyone, but that's just primitive nonsense. *(Mark Anthony, the Psychic Lawyer, author of Never Letting Go and Evidence of Eternity)*

HOW CAN I BEST HEAR MY INNER SELF'S VOICE AND KNOW MY HIGHEST PURPOSES?

ANITA MOORJANI

The best thing you can do is to just be who you are. Be true to yourself, be authentic. One of the reasons why people find this difficult is because they don't love and value themselves. When we don't value ourselves, we give our power away to other people. We think others know what's best for us. We listen to what other people tell us that we should be doing or we look at what other people are doing and want to do to better than them. We take our cues from the outside world.

What I encourage you to do is you *go inward, don't go outward*. Go inward and ask yourself, "How can I love myself more? How can I value myself more? What would bring me more joy in my life?" Listen to your own internal answers. The more you get in touch with these things, the more you get to know who you are and that's all you have to do. Be who you are because if you don't, you're depriving the world of who you came here to be. That's the reason for the title of my book, *Dying to be Me*. I had to die to learn that all I had to do is be me.

P.M.H. ATWATER

I'm a big believer in prayer and meditation. I don't think there is a better way. There are lots of ways to meditate: contemplation, being in the sunlight, and relaxing. Know that only that which is of God will come to you. Affirm that only your highest good will come to you. When you do that, great shifts in consciousness will start to occur.

If you feel led to do something, get in there with both feet and all of your heart. But if you feel led to not participate, then pull back because there are always reasons and you may not know them until later. I have learned to respect the guidance within me and I always ask, "Is it appropriate for my highest good and the highest good of all concerned if I participate?"

MARK PITSTICK

It's important to quiet your mind so you can hear your inner voice and God. Your brain is a wonderful computer, but it can't comprehend the big picture since it only senses less than one percent of reality.

That's why it's important to regularly engage in what are called *centering practices,* ways to get quiet within and realize you are one with the Universe. When you calm your mind, you get a sense of the greater reality, that life is going to work out just fine—even though it may not seem like it at the time. You remember that all life stories have a happy ending since we each are eternal beings of energy/consciousness/spirit.

Seated meditation is a great centering practice, but you don't have to sit still. *Walking meditations* involve walking in nature or in a labyrinth. If you can, regularly walk barefoot in the grass or sand to release negative energies and pick up good energy. Being around a confluence of earth, water, and wind is said to be especially beneficial. Breathing deeply and rhythmically, whether seated or walking, moves the chi, the life force/spirit that is your most true nature.

Other ways to hear your inner wisdom include prayer, yoga, chanting, drumming, music, the arts, sacred lovemaking, gardening, playing with children or pets, serving others, and knitting. Basically, try different practices that remind you it's all good, it's all God.

In my workshops, I teach several ways to listen to that still small voice within. One is *Daleth Transformational Breathwork* as taught by Tom Goode, ND, and Rusty and Tricia Barrier. I also facilitate several techniques that are done under hypnosis: *Ask Your Soul, Your Life Review*, and *Healing Your Past*. All of these approaches—available on my website as CDs—allow you to get more in touch with your inner wisdom and release old wounds and fears.

Finally, it's very difficult to hear your inner guidance when you are chronically tired, depressed, anxious, in pain, or out of balance. Fine-tune your body/mind so it's communicating and on the same wavelength as your inner self. I discuss this topic fully in my book *Radiant Wellness*. The following natural health care approaches are invaluable: specific chiropractic adjustments of the spine and skull, nutritional healing with whole food supplements, acupuncture, and deep massage. These four methods—along with optimal self-care—can *help you heal yourself* of most common mental and physical symptoms so you can become more self-aware.

MARILYN SCHLITZ

As I mentioned earlier, I have been very active in developing practices for transformation in consciousness. In our book call *Living Deeply: the Art and Science of Transformation in Everyday Life* that helped us identify a kind of *change process*. What we found is that the primary catalyst for positive, life-affirming transformation is some kind of *noetic experience*. Noetic basically means "direct knowing" involving states of insight that we don't usually put into language. These can come through self-reflection, meditation, a walk in nature, or gardening. Transformation can really be catalyzed in almost any way that allows us to shut down the weapons of mass *distraction* that bombard us all the time.

To do this we can begin to find ways to center and bring awareness to our breathing, to the sensations in our body, to what gives us inspiration, joy, and hope. Where do we find it easiest to cultivate these qualities? What allows us to create the spaciousness to define what gives us purpose and possibility in our lives?

Also important is right *livelihood*. This involves finding a job that takes care of basic needs and also provides us with growth opportunities. It's a great gift if we can take joy in our work. Having *right community* is important. If things are chaotic all the time, it's really hard on our minds and bodies. It is helpful to find places of refuge - go to a library, go for a walk in nature. Sit quietly where we can center and find the inner resilience and hardiness to be stronger in the face of transformations that come willingly or not in our lives.

Looking at the change model, we have found that this noetic inner knowing becomes fundamental to making the kinds of positive changes that we want. And then practice. Find ways to build new habits and set intentions: "I intend to have a cheerier outlook, to be in greater harmony, to own that the thoughts I'm suffering from are inflicted by myself."

How can we change those thoughts for the better? Where are we placing our attention—on the half empty or half full glass? It's also helpful to start paying attention to what we're not paying attention to. Become more mindful of all the ways in which culture conditions us.

Set some goals, little goals one at a time, and build new habits. Find guidance by listening to inspirational and educational programs. Get guidance from people who have been on the path, but also make time to be quiet and get guidance from within.

All that becomes really powerful and ultimately helps you accept life as it is, that we are part of a beautiful process that we are fundamentally part of. These methods can help people if they just slow down and reflect on what gives them purpose and meaning.

GARY SCHWARTZ

The first thing is to be open to all this being possible, to know you have a choice if you wish to do this, to have an intention to do this with genuineness and gratitude. You enter this space saying, "This is how I want to live my life and what I wish to do as an individual."

Secondly, there are various techniques for meditation, to quiet ones mind. One of the things I do personally is focus on love. "Energy flows where a loving mind goes." You can consciously put yourself into a loving mind state by doing exercises where you put one hand on your heart and one hand on your abdomen as you're breathing in. You feel the energy flowing up your left arm into your heart and think the words "love—heart." As you breathe out, you feel or imagine the energy flowing down your right arm into your right hand and think "love—breath."

You're literally filling your consciousness with love for your heart and breath. It's extremely relaxing, energizing, and takes you to the path of being love-focused. As you become more love-focused, you develop loving energy habits of mind and heart. It then becomes easier to discern and use more of your capabilities.

You could also think the words "divine love—heart" and "divine love—breath." That shifts your consciousness from just the personal notion of love to the divine. That word works particularly well for me. I've researched this with over 400 people and most say their experience is more intense and broader. They feel it more over their whole body and they connect with higher experiences.

CAROLINE MYSS

What do they think a highest purpose is? Some people reduce it to a task or an occupation instead of the quality of human being. These two things go hand in hand. You can't be someone who is dishonest and lacks a moral conscience and, at the same time, decide you want to do your highest spiritual purpose. These things X each other out.

It's simple as that. So regarding your higher purpose, you start developing yourself as a human being: your conscience, ethics, integrity, self-esteem. Then your whole sense of what you are able to do as a "higher purpose" begins to evolve in you because you become someone with the stamina to do something for others.

Higher purpose means, by its very implication, what can I do for others that makes a difference in this world? It's not about what you can do for yourself and how much attention you can get. It's about what am I capable of doing for the lives of others? But in order to do that, you have to really become someone inside who is harmless to others.

BILL GUGGENHEIM

What is your passion? What turns you on? What makes you want to get up in the morning and work on it many hours per day? What do you want to share with other people and it's not about the money—it's just for the joy of it? That's the answer about what is your life purpose. Those people who are fortunate enough to pursue their life's purpose feel most happy and joyful. They feel they aren't working, but they often get paid for it and many of them get paid remarkably well. Some of the most creative people are like that.

You can best hear your inner voice through meditation. It will give you creative ideas, lead you to places, and cause you to take risks by doing things you wouldn't do otherwise. When you take those risks, doors open and get blown off their hinges. You know you're doing the right thing for yourself and for others. And, again, it's all about love and service. When one evolves sufficiently high in love, they start becoming servers.

BERNIE SIEGEL

What impresses me is the theme of the still pond. The bird that thought it was an ugly duckling looked into the still water and realized it's a swan. Joseph Campbell talked about a tiger whose mother died giving birth to him. He was raised by goats and didn't know he was a tiger until another tiger took him to a still pond and said, "Look. You are a tiger like me!"

Yoga and meditation are excellent ways to quiet your mind, to see who you are and that's the key. If you are always thinking, worrying, giving others the power to define you, you never see yourself because there's turbulence in the pond, in the water. But when you can quiet your mind through meditation or whatever technique you use and look you'll see in the still pond who you truly are.

I also encourage people to put photographs of themselves around the home and where they work. Create little shrines, especially of yourself as a child, and love that child.Whenever you go by, you see the beauty in that child.

In my book The Art of Healing are many actual drawings from patients; this is another way to hear what the inner self is saying to us. I really feel that the reason we sleep is to give our consciousness a chance to speak to us through symbols whether they're about physical or emotional issues. The psyche and soma are one and they can speak to us. But you have to turn off your intellect to get that to happen and that's what happens when we sleep, meditate, draw, and so forth.

I have people draw pictures. I asked a male engineer to do this and he wrote a page of instructions on what needed to be drawn, but never drew a picture. That woke him up to what he was like. A lawyer said, "I came to the conclusion that I was imminently reasonable and logical, but completely wrong. While learning to think, I almost forgot how to feel."

You've got to be open to these other things so the truth can come forth to you. There are many aspects of our lives that cannot speak in words so they have to speak in symbols. When people draw pictures of themselves, they learn things that need to be corrected or enhanced. This relates to your health and everything else. Your life is stored in your body and you need to deal with issues and resolve them.

STAN GROF

Some kind of rigorous spiritual practice provides the best opportunity for us to get really profound answers about the nature of reality, our own nature, and the spiritual dimensions in the universe. It certainly can open up this whole dimension for us. Powerful experiential forms of psychotherapy, for example, holotropic breathwork that Christina and I developed at the Esalen Institute, can induce inner experiences.

And, this is not recommended, but many people have profound revelations after experiences with psychedelics. Others have spiritual emergencies, spontaneous episodes of holotropic states, that are usually diagnosed as psychotic episodes and treated with hospitalization and tranquilizers. These crises can become spiritual openings if they are properly supported and understood. They can be transformative, healing, evolutionary and bring answers to profound questions about our own nature and the nature of reality.

KAREN WYATT

To hear your inner self's voice, you have to remove any inner obstacles. The most common ones are wounds you carry from earlier in life, wounds that are still unhealed. Old grudges, resentments and anger diminish your life force. It takes energy to hold those old, negative emotions within. Heal old wounds and let go of them as completely as possible. Healing the past makes you a better vessel or channel for the wisdom that wants to manifest in you.

The next step is to be still because *the voice of your inner self is quiet*. It's a whisper. You won't be able to hear that voice if you are constantly rushing around with chattering going on in your head. Spend time every day in stillness through meditation, contemplation, or prayer. Quieting your thoughts allows your inner voice to emerge.

Journaling can also be helpful. It's a great way for your inner self to speak to you. Once you get in the habit of writing in a journal everyday, you may do some *automatic writing*. That is, your inner voice can come through in your writing if you allow space for it to happen. But that's the essential requirement: you must have space and quiet for your inner voice to be heard.

As you listen to your inner wisdom, it will nudge you toward your highest purpose. Remember that *your highest purpose occurs in the present moment*. It has to do with how you live your life in each moment. It's not a goal that you're seeking for the future, a career path, or getting more education. It is how you live your life in each and every moment. So your genuine purpose is to be your highest and best self in every moment of your life. And that requires you to live from the present moment.

MARK ANTHONY

I think that prayer and meditation are the keys. Prayer is when you talk to God, meditation is when you listen. Whether you're saying the Lord's Prayer, repeating Hail Mary, or chanting a mantra, prayer centers and focuses you. It removes stress and negativity because you're opening yourself up to the God connection. When you meditate, you clear your consciousness of distractions. During meditation, you can focus on one thing.

Your consciousness is like a blackboard. If you write down everything you think or feel, it's going to be a jumbled mess at the end of the day. Meditation quiets the mind and helps you erase that blackboard so you can focus on one thing. And that's when you can best listen to your higher self. That's when you can find what your purposes are and share them. *(Mark Anthony, the Psychic Lawyer, author of Never Letting Go and Evidence of Eternity)*

RAYMOND MOODY

Well, it's just a long process. It's just a matter of sitting down and doing it. And when you do, you start having results.

Years ago, our house needed re-wiring, but we didn't know an electrician. So my wife and I held hands by the kitchen sink and prayed for God to send us just the right electrician. I know that seems a rather mundane concern, but this is how it works I gather. The point of the prayer was, maybe there is a need out there, please send us the right person. You can plunge into the Yellow Pages or you can reflect on it and ask God.

The next morning, the phone rang. My wife Cheryl picked it up and the voice on the other end said, "Hello this is B.R. Wilson." Cheryl said, "Yes dear, what is it?" And he said, "Your number just came up on my beeper." She said, "We haven't made any calls this morning. What is this about?" He said, "I'm an electrician."

She said, "Come on over, B.R." and he did. He looked around, gave us estimates, and said, "It will be a few days before I can get out here. My brother died and my mother had a heart attack coming back from his funeral." So Cheryl said, "Maybe my husband can help you. He talks to people who have been through things like that." B.R. said, "My mother gave me this book called *Life after Life* to read and it's helping. (That was the first book Dr. Moody wrote.)

I am sure many people have had such experiences. So that's where I am with listening to my inner wisdom. I think that God interacts with us constantly.

10

HOW CAN I EVOLVE BEYOND PAST RELIGIOUS TEACHINGS THAT DON'T MAKE SENSE TO ME NOW?

EXAMPLES INCLUDE AN ETERNAL HELL, WE WERE BORN INTO SIN, THERE'S ONLY ONE TRUE RELIGION, BEING GAY IS SINFUL, ETC.

ANITA MOORJANI

Death transcends religion because everyone dies. It doesn't matter whether you're a Christian, Hindu, Buddhist, atheist… everybody dies. If you are affiliated with a religion and it works for you, great. I don't underestimate the value of religion for some people because it brings them comfort, community, and a way to serve others. Any religion or belief also needs to empower you. If it brings you fear, if it makes you feel small or discouraged, then it's time to reevaluate.

I have nothing against religion per se, but I'm more interested in people as individuals expressing who they are. I have a problem with people who kill each other in the name of religion or judge others for any reason. If you are outgrowing your religion, but don't want to leave that community, start to show

---

people a better way. Don't fight against it. The best thing you can do is be who you are, be an inspiration, and lead by example. Be passionate about your new beliefs and teach others.

P.M.H. ATWATER

Over two-thirds of people who have a near-death experience come back unable to return to the traditional church. But those who stay in the church are really excited because they want to help change the church, to give it new energy. And most of the two-thirds who leave the church are back again within about 10 years, but they join a different kind of church, mostly metaphysical churches. Or they find different ways of reaching God, for example, by praying in groups because they like to be around those of a like mind.

While we're talking about religion, after my near-death experiences, I was drawn to *Unity, Science of Mind* and *Religious Science* churches because those really spoke to me. I went back to church because I liked the group. I liked the idea of a community of souls. I didn't go back to find God. I'd already done that.

MARK PITSTICK

In what other area of life today do people rely upon millennia old information? Not for healthcare, technology, or transportation—but many do with their beliefs about soul, God, and the afterlife.

I encourage a dialogue within the church so it becomes stronger and more responsive to people's needs. I attended theological school and learned for myself that *The Bible* has been changed mightily over the centuries through numerous translations, interpretations, deletions, and additions. Then, as now, powerful men controlled these teachings to increase their power and fortune.

That's one reason why religious teachings may not resonate with your inner voice. Over the years, many older people have told me that, as children, they could never believe horrific teachings about judgment and hell. I encourage people to recognize that holy books may have been inspired by God, but they were certainly written and changed by humans. Over time, their teachings were concretized and became doctrines.

When I was writing *Soul Proof*, I called churches of several different denominations and asked, "What does your church believe about hell?" One of the ministers said, "Our canons from the fifteenth century clearly state that there is a fiery eternal hell for unrepentant sinners." I said, "I know that's what they believed in medieval times, but what does your church believe now?" There was a long pause and he said, "We still go by those canons." And I thought, "Oh my God. They called that time period the Dark Ages for good reasons."

I'll give churches the benefit of the doubt and say that, in the past, they were doing the best they could with what they knew at the time. But now there's *new information* that needs to be recognized. I recommend that people sift through religious teachings and keep what makes sense while letting go of the rest. Thomas Jefferson said the truth is embedded in *The Bible* like diamonds in a dung heap and I have to agree with him. So sift through it, use what makes sense to you and let go of what doesn't.

Only 19 percent of Americans regularly attend church these days. In the past, some churches weren't open to people of other races, different faiths, those in interracial marriages, gays, divorced people, etc. It's gotten better but there's still room for improvement, especially among the more fundamentalist denominations.

But churches also do a lot of good by serving people with many outreaches. Rather than throwing out the baby with the bath water, perhaps it's time for change from within. Fortunately, some churches are becoming more open and responsive to people's needs and contemporary evidence.

One nice thing about an evidence-based spiritual perspective is that we can now release needless concerns that God is a huge vengeful dictator who's going smite us and send us to hell forever if we question traditional teachings. We now can look at life's biggest questions with a clearer perspective and without fear.

It's time to quit looking at outward differences and realize we are all children of God and we are one with the One right now. Churches that do this will grow. I recommend that people learn from the contemporary afterlife evidence, their inner wisdom, and religious teachings that make sense to them.

MARILYN SCHLITZ

Through the research that I've done on worldly transformation and living deeply, I found there is an important kind of literacy I call *worldview literacy*. It's the awareness that we all have a worldview and that we can cultivate practices to help us better understand what that worldview is. What informs it? What limits it? These are skill sets that we can learn. We've actually built a curriculum called *worldview explorations* that can help to facilitate that.

Then there's the idea that other people have a worldview that's different from our own. It may or may not be right, but it's different. There are ways in which different worldviews can cause us to become reactive. *Amygdala hijacking* can occur when the old fight-or-flight part of the brain gets triggered before we're even consciously aware of it.

To the extent we can become more aware of those triggers within, we can then develop the capacity to be less reactive in the face of different views.

There are skills we can develop to make us *more curious and creative* in response to differences. Having a full range of worldviews can be very healthy. Ultimately, how does our worldview lead to actions in the world so we live with meaning and purpose, in ways that are full, rich and juicy? My websites (*www.marilynschlitz.com* and *www.deathmakeslifepossible.com*), and my workshops offer resources so people can take steps and see what comes up for them.

GARY SCHWARTZ

First of all, we have to understand that most of our religions arose many thousands of years ago. These people did the best they could with the knowledge they had, which was minimal. They believed that the Earth was flat, that the sun revolves around the Earth. People used to have all kinds of beliefs that were quite naive by today's standards.

It's not surprising that our spirituality is going to change as our knowledge grows. So first of all, we have to forgive our churches, temples, and mosques. We have to forgive the writings of people who hadn't progressed beyond ancient historical views of their time.

Secondly, we have to stay open-minded. There are grains of truth in almost every spiritual tradition. We can celebrate the genuineness of people who were on those paths, but still treat them as historical. I believe we need to develop *evidence-based faith*—not faith based on history and dogma—that supports an evolving spirituality.

In fact, there's a new website called *www.eternea.org* founded by Dr. Eban Alexander, who wrote *Proof of Heaven,* and John Audette. It's a convergence of science and spirituality; they offer seven spiritual postulates that are based on scientific evidence. These postulates are also corner stones of most religions. They're trying to develop and expand our spiritual understandings that are also supported by science. Science is not taking away spirituality, it's actually taking us to spirituality. This is really wonderful; we can evolve as individuals and, at the same time, be respectful of traditions we were raised in.

All of us have to grow. If that means we have to change some of the religious teachings we once believed were true, so be it. We all thought the sun revolved around the Earth and we were all wrong. That's okay. The critical thing is that we can always learn and grow.

CAROLINE MYSS

That takes work because those are superstitions that run thick and deep in a person's grain. They really do. And I don't think people realize how strong of a hold superstitions have on them—much more so, in fact, than faith and a belief in God. You learn fear much sooner than you learn faith. People are fearful of change and are frightened to speak the truth, to think the truth, to hear the truth.

So it takes a lot of conscious effort. You've got to pay attention to yourself. There's nothing about inner growth that is not a lot of work. You almost need a self-exorcism combined with a profound commitment to inner reflection and prayer. You've got to put both together and pay attention to what has you under a spell.

BILL GUGGENHEIM

I don't think you can really push evolution on others, you just have to evolve in your own way. So if one religion or philosophy doesn't make sense, you become open to something else that does. You find yourself watching a different TV show like Wayne Dyer on PBS or picking up a new book. You'll go to a yoga or spirituality class and meet new people. It's not just changing your beliefs, it's a new way of life that you're stepping into. You can't hold on to the old. You have to be willing to meet new people with new interests, resources and activities. It's kind of like moving from place to another, but you're moving internally.

For those who would like to change organized religion from within, I wish them well. In most churches, I would be excommunicated. I just finished reading a book by an Episcopalian priest who interviewed a minister who used to work for a very conservative Christian church. The minister preached about sin and hell-fire damnation all the time and, the more he did, the more the congregation grew. Then this minister had a near-death experience. He came back and said, "Oops, I was all wrong. It's about love, forgiveness, sharing and caring." After that, the congregation immediately began to diminish. Some people want to hear about the negative stuff and others don't.

If you want to try to do the impossible and roll a large rock up a mountain like Sisyphus, try doing in it in a large orthodox church. It ain't going to happen. You can try but, in my humble opinion, you're not going to get much in the way of results.

BERNIE SIEGEL

I've been called satanic and occult by a minister in Mississippi because I taught visual imagery. The minister said Satan could take over your images. When people are fundamentalists, words are their God. They need security in their interpretations. What I like is to sit and debate it. In Judaism they'll do that. They'll take some statement and say "What do you think God meant?" and then they look into it. So you are not stuck in some interpretation that, "It means this, it means that." What bothers me about religion is the guilt, the shame, the blame that they heap on people.

I like to think of religion as a guide book; I like reading about all the religions. We are one family and that's what we need to understand. It's not about religion and separation. It's about coming together and becoming one.

STAN GROF

When you asked before about how people experience the Divine, I described a radiant source of energy, intelligence and creativity and also a pregnant void. And then you mentioned the archaic image of God as an old man sitting on a throne. My experience of the Divine is echoed by mystics from different religions. But organized religions deal more with images, not experiences. Joseph Campbell's comment was very interesting when he said, "A useful deity should be transparent for the transcendent." If you make it opaque, they start worshiping specific images, what is called idolatry.

This is what you find very frequently in organized religions when a group of people decides to worship these particular images in certain ways. You then have a religion that unites a certain group of people, but divides the world and creates dichotomies: We are Christians, you are pagans. Everybody should be a Christian. We are Muslims, you are infidels. Everybody should be a Muslim. We are Jews, we are Sikhs, we are Hindus, and on and on. These images of hell and heaven are part of the archetypal world and different religions have different descriptions of heaven and hell.

What is important is the self-expression *to move beyond* the images to the Source out of which everything comes. Then religion becomes what it should be: something that binds together what appears to be fragmented. Self-exploration helps us release past unconscious experiences that were hellish so we're not threatened by fire-and-brimstone preachers.

KAREN WYATT

I would view this as *transcending* religious teachings that served a purpose for you at some point in the past. Those teachings may have made sense earlier as you were developing spiritually. But as you evolve, they may not work for you anymore. Hold in mind a vision of rising above the teachings that don't fit now.

It's much the same as getting rid of clothes that don't fit you anymore. You give them to someone since you are going to be clothed in something new. You are transcending old teachings and opening to higher forms of wisdom. But don't throw away everything you learned from past religious teachings. Some of what you learned is still important and valuable, especially the parts about love and forgiveness.

MARK ANTHONY

I'm a proponent of religion, but religion must never be used as a moral justification for anger, bigotry, hatred and violence. Muslim terrorists scream that Allah wants them to reap death and destruction, but nothing could be further from the truth and core teachings of Islam. Religious fanatics parade around as Christians and use fear-based superstitions to try to prosecute an entire group of people such as gays. It's really sad because Jesus spoke about peace and love and understanding. He taught us to treat others the way they would want to be treated. He said that if you do not know love, you do not know God—for God is love. He taught that the word of God is for everyone, not just a particular group of people. He brought a universal message of non-violence.

I get all these hateful comments on my Facebook page, pretty much every day, from "good Christians." They quote from Deuteronomy and Leviticus that mediums are not of God and say, "I believe in the Scriptures; you're evil."

Well, those Old Testament chapters also say that if your daughter enters a temple while she's menstruating, she must be put to death. Or if your neighbor works on the Sabbath, you should have him put to death. And much more. I really hope that these fanatics are not taking all that literally.

When I hear, 'There is only one way to God,' I'm like... really? We're talking about an intelligence that created the universe, maybe multi-verses, and realms we can't even comprehend. And you're saying that all of creation, from a subatomic to an universal or cosmic level, should be interpreted by millennia-old teachings of one culture? This is especially hard to understand when you realize these ancient teachings have been edited by innumerable ecumenical counsels, religious squabbling, and political compromise.

I encourage people to get beyond the fear and ignorance and embrace what Jesus, Buddha, Krishna and others were really talking about: peace, love, and understanding. Every religion has a Golden Rule. Religion is a path to God and there are as many potential paths to God as there are people in the world. *(Mark Anthony, the Psychic Lawyer, author of Never Letting Go and Evidence of Eternity)*

RAYMOND MOODY

What a scary thing. I am writing a book called *God Is Bigger Than the Bible* and it's about twelve ideas I have about God. One of them is that God doesn't care whether we join a religion. It's fascinating to me that billions of people think God is encouraging or requiring them to join some particular religion. But they can't quite get an agreement about which one since different people join different religions.

I didn't grow up with religion. My mother's mother poked humor at religion, but very gently. My Dad was very secular about it. Number one, he was a surgeon and everyone probably knows that personality. Number two, he was a professional military officer and served in the Pacific theater as a medic in WWII. His generation didn't talk much, but I just gathered that what he saw must have been horror after horror. Religion offered nothing for him. I grew up thinking that religion was laughable; I am sorry to be so blunt but I am sixty-nine years old.

God has never said a word to me about religion. I consult him about life several times a day and I know some of His ways. He gives me direction about all kinds of things but doesn't communicate about religion. I think to Him it must be a topic of some hilarity because the whole picture is just so funny. I don't think that God requires us to join a religion and I don't think He really cares about that. I really don't.

11 HOW CAN THIS INFORMATION HELP ME BETTER HANDLE MY TOUGHEST CHALLENGES AND MAKE THE WORLD A BETTER PLACE NOW?

ANITA MOORJANI

When we know who we are and express our authentic selves, the challenges we face are in line with our purpose. We bring them on ourselves and we grow from these problems. Sometimes, we deal with challenges that are not ours because we're so busy trying to be somebody who we are not. We're listening to advertisers that make us feel, "If we don't have this, we're nobody." We buy stuff we can't afford. Trying to live a life that is not ours brings problems that are not ours; then don't know how to cope with it.

When you learn to love and value yourself, when you allow yourself to be authentic, you will still have challenges, but those will be of your own making. Overcoming those challenges will lead to growth and you will find gifts in those challenges. That's just one reason why it's so important to be who you are. When you truly express who you really are, your best life will unfold before you.

When we realize that the answers lie within and when we see God within ourselves, we don't have to go out and convince anyone of anything. The minute you're faced with other people, you see the same God looking out from behind their eyes. You don't feel the need to go and fight to change the world; your very presence changes it. Be the change you want to see in the world as Gandhi said. Be it so that where ever you go, there you are.

Many believe that we need to fight for our causes, but that just makes us more angry. We get angry at government, medical systems, large corporations. Wherever we go, we take our angry selves and create more defensiveness and furor. To see more peace, be it and share it.

We are seeing more and more cancer in the world and it's partly because we are so focused on illness. We spend many billions of dollars on cancer awareness campaigns, research, earlier detection, and so on. Just imagine if we put that same amount of awareness, money, and resources on *wellness awareness*. Most people and medical providers don't even know what that means. If more people became aware of what it means to be truly well, we would see a very different world and a very different result. The same goes for world peace and so on.

P.M.H. ATWATER

Well, you don't stay down long, you bounce back. You're still living life one day at a time and going through the tough times. Many near-death experiencers come back facing bouts of depression and confusion because they can't handle being back on earth. After a near-death experience, it's tough to realize what happened to you and what you can do about it. It takes a while to get your confidence back and live with those new understandings.

For me, every day became a test or an opportunity to use what I knew to be true. That approach works consistently. Do I still have down times? Of course.

When that happens, I say "OK, here's a new opportunity for learning" and I turn it around.

That is what a lot of us do. When tough times come along—whether an automobile accident, losing a child, whatever it is—stop, take a deep breath and swallow. When you do that, it clears the brain and heart. You're able to take the next step and that step can be positive. You're able to see that no matter what is happening, you can deal with it. You can walk through it.

After I died, I went through a lot of fear. I had to relearn how to crawl, stand, climb stairs, tell the difference between left and right, see properly, hear properly and rebuild all my belief systems. And I learned this mantra: "Fear is the mind killer. I will face my fears. And after they have passed over, around, and through me, I will remain."

We make the world a better place by making ourselves better. You can't change somebody else, the only person you can change is yourself. When I change myself, I automatically start changing things around me. It's like taking a pebble and dropping it into a lake, you have all these ripples. So when you change yourself, you are changing the world because we are the world, we are co-creators with Creator.

MARK PITSTICK

Where do I begin? So many benefits exist to really knowing that you—and everyone else—are indestructible beings of energy/spirit/consciousness who are integral parts of Source Energy *right now*. Here's a partial list:

- Death is not an end, just a new beginning to the next phase of forever

- You will see your departed loved ones again and can do so now

- There is a meaning, a rhyme and reason, to all life's events even if you can't see it now from your limited earthly perspective

- You have unique gifts to share and others need them

- You are not a failure or sinner since you learn by "mistakes;" it is important, however, to truly repent: apologize, make amends, and do better the next time

- There are no eternal hells, just temporary, self-chosen ones

- You will benefit greatly by caring for your body/mind—the temple of your soul

- You have everything you need to handle all of life's changes and challenges with style… even if it doesn't seem like it

- This information doesn't take away all the grief and sadness when you face a tragedy or death of a loved one, but it doesn't lighten it immeasurably

- You can always improve the quality of your life—no matter what your current situation or what is going on around you

MARILYN SCHLITZ

We can connect to our communities and involve ourselves in different kinds of projects that bring us into the world. We can begin to see that life is a daily practice, not just something we do on special days at special times, but every moment... in our carpool, a difficult situation, or at the workplace. Those are all opportunities for us. I like to think of road rage situations as a potential spiritual practice because we get the opportunity to check our own reactiveness.

Sometimes a little reminder in our car helps—whether it's a bobble-headed Buddha, Christ figure, or smiley face.

These little reminders can be very important. So, first of all, we work on ourselves. Second, we engage in our communities in whatever form that takes. Reaching out and connecting is really important. Systems—whether education, health care, business, community, religion—all have the capacity to change. And the best way to change is from the inside-out, using principles of the transformational model to affect *whole systems change*. One person at a time can help lead to a shift in a critical mass of people, a tipping point. That's where I believe we're at right now, especially with mass communications and more people asking the kinds of questions you're asking, then answering them in ways that can help create new forms of action.

GARY SCHWARTZ

Singers and composers such as John Denver, John Lennon, and Michael Jackson addressed evolving our spirituality. The song "Man in the Mirror" says that if we wish to contribute to solving humanity's greatest problems, including the mess we've made of the planet, it has to begin within. We have to look at ourselves in the mirror first and decide that we're going to change ourselves. And as we grow and change, we can then contribute to others.

Whether we get our inspiration from spiritual leaders, scientists or entertainers, the critical thing is that we realize we're each infinite beings of energy. This is really true and, once we remember our core essence, it changes the way we see everything. It changes the way we approach life. We stop thinking of ourselves as limited beings suffering on our small planet. We realize there is a greater reality that we're each part of. We can get rid of conventional teachings and see with greater wisdom. This provides hope and inspiration. It expands our capacity to love, to be of service, to see the bigger picture.

I was invited to become the new chairman of this organization Eternea. org and was speaking with the CEO and president. I said, "The initiative of Eternea is very important. I don't just think as my life in terms of ten or twenty more years on this planet. I do envision the soul phone coming along. I'll make a deal with you. I'm willing to become the chairman, but only if we make a commitment to be of service to this particular organization for the next two hundred years."

Now, I don't mean in the physical. I don't expect to be living physically in my body for two hundred years. I just don't anticipate that. But what I do anticipate is that I can continue to be of service from "the other side" particularly as more bridges between Earth and there get built. That's just one example of how taking a longer view in our lives changes the way we live in daily moments.

CAROLINE MYSS

How can it not help you? Decide you need to do better, to see your life in a clearer direction, and pick one thing. Never start with doing everything because you'll fail. You have to start with one thing and that inevitably is attached to everything. What if you decide the one thing you're going to do is not betray yourself anymore? If you don't betray yourself, it's going to be very hard for you to betray another person.

If you say, "That's it. I'm no longer going to betray myself" and make a promise to not eat bad food, you have to stick with that. You have to stick with that because you're not going to betray what you just said to yourself. If a good friend says to you, "I want to tell you this. Would you keep this to yourself?" you have to do that because you just gave someone your word. You can't betray yourself; that means you can't betray your friend, you can no longer lie. You want your highest potential? Become your highest potential. It's not given to you, you become it. It's who you are.

You become driven and controlled by grace, by true power. You hold your center so you don't hemorrhage your power. That's your highest potential, to have control over yourself instead of others. You decide that your life is not about controlling others; that's what a weak and frightened person does. Inner control, that's what makes all the difference. And add prayer to that.

BILL GUGGENHEIM

My spiritual teachings have come through so many different teachers and teachings. I don't use just one source or book. This information has made my life much simpler and easier. I'm more confident in my perspectives about the challenges of life. I have a purpose that I never had before. Most of all, I'm better able to help other people with widely different backgrounds.

Knowing all this has helped greatly with my daughter Janet's passing. It lightened the grief. I have two daughters and a different special song with each one. The song that I associate with Janet is "Here Comes the Sun" by the Beatles. When she was living on Earth, I often thought about that song and played it and suggested that maybe she needed more sunshine in her life to make her happier. After she died, her mother created a website for her and people wrote messages on the website regarding their relationship to Janet. Reading those, I realized how much she had been there to help others and she herself was the sun that she sent to so many other people.

I started to play that song on *YouTube* one morning and, right in front of my forehead, I saw her dancing in color and I felt her motions. I heard her voice, she was speaking to me by telepathy. Her spiritual body was twirling in a circle and, at the same time, she was dancing in a larger circle. She was letting me know that she is fine, even though she used a gun to end her physical body. She is doing very well and is happy.

I learned that she is working with children by creating art. Janet's thing was art. They are able to create art in three-dimensional reality just by the power of their minds. They can make it as large as they want with different colors and any shape. She's working with the children and they, in turn, are working with her. It's a two-way relationship and it was very joyous.

And this information can make the world a better place, no doubt about it. The more loving and accepting we become, the more we serve and help other people. And, one by one, the world becomes a better place. It's that simple.

BERNIE SIEGEL

As we journey through our time on Earth, we must keep asking ourselves, "What am I to learn from this experience?" Then, like hunger, it leads us to seek and find nourishment that improves our lives. What seems like a curse then becomes a blessing just as charcoal becomes a diamond under pressure. Our consciousness does not cease to exist when our body dies. Thus, the wiser we become, the wiser those who come after us will be because of their exposure to our consciousness.

STAN GROF

On the individual level, after you have the experience of your own divinity, you then return to your everyday life, but you have a broader perspective, a sort of meta-framework. When things get tough, you can refer to insights from your spiritual states. That makes things easier to deal with. You also have a history of intense experiences that are far more powerful than what everyday life usually brings.

On the collective level, you can see a transformation that goes on independently in different people when they have this information. They experience a great reduction of aggressive, negative feelings. They develop compassion, a sense of oneness with nature and other people. They have a vision of a global community and want to transcend differences whether they are related to race, gender, nationality and so on. And there is a sense of deep unity with creation that creates an ethical responsibility. That changes what we do in the world, how we deal with other people, and how we treat nature. They almost become a different species.

And, of course, if these people start as atheists, then this kind of information can lead to a spiritual opening. Hopefully, a community of mystics will develop to the magnitude of organized religions—mystics because they don't have great problems with each other.

KAREN WYATT

That's the whole point of what we are doing here on Earth. The suffering and challenges that exist on earth can help us learn and grow. The first step is to *embrace* those difficulties and recognize them as opportunities to help us become who we are truly meant to be. One pathway to your purpose, to why you are here on Earth, is through life's suffering and challenges. *Learn to accept what is* instead of trying to remove it from your life. That helps the soul evolve and become more authentic, compassionate and courageous.

The second step is to *love and live in love* no matter what is going on in your life. Even when you feel depleted and depressed by challenges, the goal is to be the most loving being you can.

Living a life of love also requires *forgiveness*. You cannot reach the highest levels of loving without being able to forgive. Those you love will eventually hurt or disappoint you in some way. Forgiveness helps you evolve spiritually and develop a higher capacity for love. So love and forgiveness are two keys for spiritual growth in the face of difficulties.

Another key is to learn how to stay in the present moment. Manifesting your highest potential requires living in the present moment. You also need to let go of your expectations without being attached to what you wanted, hoped for, or wished would happen. Life usually doesn't turn out the way we think it will. Surrender expectations and attachments so you can *become a clear channel* for the divine love and power that wants to flow through you.

The ultimate acceptance is that your physical life on this planet is meant to come to an end. Life is set up that way. Life is a cycle of birth and death. When we reach the end of our days here, our physical bodies will die. That is a normal and beautiful aspect of living on this planet. One day, we will lose everything that we can see, feel, and touch. That knowledge helps us live more fully in the moment and enjoy all of life.

How can these insights help me make the world a better place? By living your life the way I have been describing: loving, forgiving, accepting, being present.

This helps you be an open channel so our evolutionary Creator can work through you. You become a better instrument of creativity and help solve some of the problems of the world. But you have to let go of what you think your life should be about or what you want your life to be about. This makes you a better conduit for the creative impulses that want to come through you.

The world needs what you have to offer right now. We're having so many struggles on our planet because *not enough people are awake*. Not enough people are allowing their gifts to flow creatively to make the Earth a better place. As you awaken, you make our world a better place every single moment.

More and more people are awakening. Our planet and problems will heal when we reach a critical mass of people who are pure vessels for the creative energy coming through them.

I think we have to look at the philosophical basis of all the major world religions: treat other people the way you would want to be treated. I like something that Golda Meir said, 'There will be peace in the Middle East when our Arab neighbors realize they love their children more than they hate us.' I like what Gandhi said, 'What religion is God? We're all children of God. Why do you raise your hand against your brothers and sisters simply because they call God by another name?'

When you look at great spiritual teachers—Buddha, Jesus, Gandhi, Mother Teresa, Paramahansa Yogananda, Saint Frances of Assisi, and others—they're the ones who really got it. They realized you don't use religion to bolster a political agenda. Religion can help remove anger and hatred from people. When you start looking at life the way these great teachers did, then you will have peace.

(Mark Anthony, the Psychic Lawyer, author of Never Letting Go and Evidence of Eternity)

AFTERWORD

I hope our answers help you better handle life's changes and challenges. If internalized and acted upon, this information can deepen your realization that life truly is a totally safe and magnificent adventure amidst forever.

Remembering this will lessen your feelings that you are a helpless victim in a chaotic and unjust world. To the contrary, you're a hero/heroine in a remarkably supportive and loving Universe. You're a timeless and deathless being of energy that revels in serving, growing, and enjoying many facets of life here and in the hereafter. And really knowing that, my friend, changes the whole ball game.

Remember Stevie, the little boy who was abused to death? Looking back to that time so long ago, it and other experiences were clearly "wake-up" moments for me. They were spiritually transcendent experiences that forced me to reexamine everything I had been taught about life. How many others were touched by his death and motivated to make the world a better place? We'll never know from our limited earthly perspectives, but his short life and tragic death had profound meaning and impact. And that's what his soul planned to do.

I know it's difficult to maintain this higher perspective at times. Life on Earth can be so difficult and the illusion that physicality is all there is can be so convincing. Seeing past the pain and beyond the illusion allows you to make your life a work of art. Just as one candle can light millions of others, your light can remind others about their true nature.

Life on this planet can be so rich, beautiful, and wonderful—especially when you are spiritually awakened. Developing a cosmic perspective helps you handle whatever comes along. The old saying "God never gives you more than you can handle" is true even though it might not seem like it at times. That was one of the last things my dad said before he died.

The information in this book can help you become an awakened human. You can increasingly know and show that there is much more to life than this temporary human experience. You can live with one foot in the physical world and the other in spiritual realms. That's when the game of life becomes really interesting and fun—no matter what is going on around you.

Remember to use consciousness-raising and holistic health care practices to widen the pinhole you are looking through. That will expand your perspective so you can always see the big picture, especially during life's sad and bad times. It will also increase your energy and balance so you can best handle all of life's changes and challenges with style.

In the *Boy Scouts*, our motto was "Be Prepared." You are now better prepared for life here and in the hereafter. Just notice how your life gets better with these great answers to life's most important questions and the life-transformative strategies you've learned.

Finally, thank you for sharing our answers and yours with others. Just imagine how far reaching the ripples of that dialogue will be.

GUEST BIOGRAPHIES

ANITA MOORJANI

If the doctors had been right, Anita Moorjani would not be alive today.

Now a *New York Times* best-selling author of the book *Dying to be Me*, and a world-renowned international speaker, doctors had given her mere hours to live on the morning of February 2, 2006. Unable to move, and in a deep coma caused by the cancer that had ravaged her body for nearly four years, Anita tells of entering another realm where she experienced great clarity and understanding of her life and purpose here on earth. In that realm, she was given a choice of whether to return to life or continue on into death. Anita chose to return to this life when she realized that "heaven" is a state, not a place. This awareness subsequently resulted in a remarkable and complete recovery of her health within weeks of coming out of the coma.

Born in Singapore of Indian parents, Anita has lived in Hong Kong most of her life. From the age of two, she grew up speaking English, Cantonese, and an Indian dialect simultaneously. She had been working in the corporate field for several years before her cancer diagnosis in 2002.

Shortly after her full recovery, Moorjani shared her story of healing and the insights she gained from her experience in the other realm. Moorjani's story went viral on the internet and created enormous interest on an international scale.

Her subsequent book, *Dying to be Me*, was published in March of 2012 by Hay House Publishing, and within two weeks of it's release, it hit the New York Times' bestsellers list and remained on the list for 9 weeks.

Dying to Be Me became number 1 in Canada, and was in the top 20 on the Canadian book charts for six months. It has been translated into 42 languages and has sold over 1 million copies worldwide.

Following the worldwide success of her book, Anita has regularly been interviewed on various prime-time television shows around the world, including CNN's *Anderson Cooper 360, Fox News* in New York, *The Jeff Probst Show* in Hollywood, cable TV's *National Geographic International*, *The Today Show* with Maria Shriver, *The Pearl Report* in Hong Kong, *HeadStart* with Karen Davila in the Philippines, among many others. She travels the globe speaking at conferences.

In February 2015, *Scott Free Productions* - owned by internationally acclaimed Hollywood producer Ridley Scott, have optioned the rights to make *Dying To Be* Me into a full-length feature film.

Website: *www.anitamoorjani.com*

Facebook: *https://facebook.com/Anita.Moorjani*

Tweet: *@AnitaMoorjani*

P.M.H. ATWATER, L.H.D.

Atwater is one of the original researchers in the field of near-death studies, having begun her work in 1978. Some of her findings have been verified in clinical studies, among them a prospective study conducted in Holland and published in *Lancet* medical journal 12-15-01. Her book *The Big Book of Near-Death Experiences (Rainbow Ridge Books, 2014)* covers the field globally, and is the only encyclopedia of the entire phenomenon. It was featured in an online version of Newsweek Magazine.

She was presented the Outstanding Service Award in 2005 from the International Association for Near-Death Studies (IANDS), and the Lifetime Achievement Award from the National Association of Transpersonal Hypnotherapists (NATH). In 2009, she was given the Nancy E. Bush award for Literary Excellence and the Lifetime Achievement and Special Services Award, both from IANDS.

She is an international speaker and has been a guest on numerous television shows including Geraldo, Regis and Kathie Lee, Larry King Live, Sally Jessy Raphael, and Entertainment Tonight. Dr. Atwater's books have been translated into over 12 languages. Some of her other books are:
Dying to Know You: Proof of God in the Near-Death Experience (Rainbow Ridge Books, 2014) – based on thousands of people who died clinically, what they went through and learned, and how they came back to a world that no longer made sense to them.

Near-Death Experiences: The Rest of The Story (Hampton Roads, 2011) – discusses 33 years of field work involving sessions with nearly 4,000 adult and child experiencers of near-death states.

Future Memory (Hampton Roads, updated in 2013) – explores consciousness and unusual aftereffects of near-death and other transformative states. Written in a pattern that duplicates the layout and feeling of a labyrinth.

The New Children and Near-Death Experiences (Bear & Co., 2003) – the only book that looks in-depth, and from the child's viewpoint, at pediatric near-death states. Covers pre-birth and birth trauma cases and their evolutionary aspects.

Children of the Fifth World (Bear & Co., 2012) – considers why today's children in general are so much like child experiencers of near-death states. Focuses on evolutionary issues with today's children and our rapidly changing times.

A near-death experiencer herself, her book *I Died Three Times in 1977* can be purchased on Amazon.com. Her DVD/CD, *As You Die*, was developed to guide the dying through physical death and the soul's separation as it occurs and is available from her online bookstore at www.pmhatwater.com. Her book, *We Live Forever: The Real Truth About Death*, is available through the A.R.E. Press.

Website: *www.pmhatwater.com*

MARILYN SCHLITZ, PH.D.

Dr. Schlitz is a social anthropologist, researcher, writer, and charismatic public speaker. She is currently the Founder and CEO of Worldview Enterprises. She also serves as President Emeritus and a Senior Fellow at the Institute of Noetic Sciences. Additionally, she is a Senior Scientist at the California Pacific Medical Center, where she focuses on health and healing, and board member of Pacifica Graduate Institute.

For more than three decades, Marilyn has been a leader in the field of consciousness studies. Her research and extensive publications focus on personal and social transformation, cultural pluralism, extended human capacities, and mind body medicine.

She has a depth of leadership experience in government, business, and the not-for-profit sectors. Her broad and varied work has given her a unique ability to help individuals and organizations identify and develop personal and interpersonal skills and capacities needed by 21st century leaders.

She recently wrote and produced a feature film called *Death Makes Life Possible* with Deepak Chopra on the topic of death and dying, and how engaging that topic in a deep and meaningful way informs the way we live our lives.

Her books include: *Living Deeply, the Art and Science of Transformation in Everyday Life, Consciousness and Healing: Integral Approaches to Mind-Body Medicine*, and *Worldview Explorations Workbook*.

Marilyn is a dynamic and experienced public speaker, teacher, and trainer. She combines culture, science, and spirituality in an original, engaging and compelling style. She has a rare gift to translate complex ideas into a form that is easily accessible. Schlitz has lectured in many venues, including the United Nations, the Smithsonian Institute, and many conferences.

Website: *www.marilynschlitz.com*

GARY E. SCHWARTZ, PH.D.

Dr. Schwartz is Professor of Psychology, Medicine, Neurology, Psychiatry, and Surgery at the University of Arizona. In addition to teaching courses on health psychology and the psychology of religion and spirituality, he is the director of the Laboratory for Advances in Consciousness and Health.

He received a nearly two million-dollar award from the National Center on Complementary and Alternative Medicine of the National Institutes of Health to create a Center for Frontier Medicine in Biofield Science at the University of Arizona, which he directed for four years.

Gary collaborates with Canyon Ranch on biofield science and energy healing research and serves as the Corporate Director of Development of Energy Healing. He also serves as Chairman of Eternea, an organization whose mission is to foster the integration of science and spirituality for personal and global transformation (www.eternea.org).

Gary received his Ph.D. in psychology from Harvard University in 1971 and was an assistant professor at Harvard for five years. He later served as a professor of psychology and psychiatry at Yale University, director of the Yale Psychophysiology Center, and co-director of the Yale Behavioral Medicine Clinic, before moving to Arizona in 1988.

He has published more than four hundred and fifty scientific papers, including six papers in the journal *Science*. Gary has also co-edited eleven academic books. He is the author of *The Sacred Promise* (2011), *The Energy*

Healing Experiments (2007), *The G.O.D. Experiments* (2006), *The Afterlife Experiments* (2002), *The Truth about Mediums* (2005), and *The Living Energy Universe* (1999).

Gary is a Fellow of the American Psychological Association, the American Psychological Society, the Society for Behavioral Medicine, and the Academy for Behavioral Medicine Research. He has received many awards for distinguished research and was the founding President of the Forever Family Foundation, a non-profit organization that fosters research and education on afterlife science and healing. (www.foreverfamilyfoundation.org)

He frequently speaks about health psychology, energy healing, and spiritual research and has been interviewed on many major network television and radio shows. His work has been the subject of documentaries and profiles on *Discovery, HBO,* the *SciFi Channel, Arts & Entertainment, Fox* and others. His research was featured on the *The Life After Death Project.* www.lifeafterdeathproject.com His work has been described in various magazines and newspapers including *USA Today,* the *London Times, The New York Times, The LA Times,* and others.

Website: *www.drgaryschwartz.com*

CAROLINE MYSS, M.A.

Caroline is a five-time *New York Times* bestselling author and internationally renowned speaker in the fields of human consciousness, spirituality and mysticism, health, energy medicine, and the science of medical intuition. In addition to hosting a weekly radio show on the Hay House network, Caroline maintains a rigorous international workshop and lecture schedule.

After completing her Master's degree, Caroline co-founded *Stillpoint Publishing*. Simultaneously, she refined her skills as a medical intuitive, with the assistance of C. Norman Shealy, M.D., Ph.D., a Harvard-trained neurosurgeon. Caroline developed the field of Energy Anatomy, a science that correlates specific emotional/physical/ psychological/spiritual stress patterns with diseases. Her research became the subject matter of a book co-written by her and Norm: *The Creation of Health.*

In 1996, Caroline released *Anatomy of the Spirit.* Through the investigation of the underlying reasons why people sabotage their healing processes, Caroline identified a syndrome she calls "woundology," characterized by a person's reliance on the power of illness for manipulation of his or her world, as opposed to attaining an independent, empowered state of health. Her third book is *Why People Don't Heal and How They Can.*

Caroline then pursued her interest in the language of symbols, myths, and archetypes, conducting research that enabled her to profile an individual's "Sacred Contract," a complex of 12 archetypal patterns that reflect in mythic language the agreements the soul made prior to birth. Based on this work, Caroline released *Sacred Contracts,* which became her third New York Times bestseller.

Caroline followed with *Invisible Acts of Power* in 2004 and *Entering the Castle* in 2007. *Defy Gravity,* a book exploring the mystical phenomenon of healing that transcends reason, was released in 2009.

In 2003, Oprah Winfrey gave Caroline her own television program with the OXYGEN network in New York City, which ran successfully for one year. In addition to her written work, Caroline has produced more than eighty audio/visual products on subjects that include healing, spirituality, personal development, and archetypes.

Most recently, Caroline has joined forces with Archetypeme.com, a state-of-the-art web company that is dedicated to creating a global community by helping people connect to each other through their individual archetypes. Her newest book, *Archetypes: Who Are You?* brings archetypes into the mainstream, introducing the public to how they can identify their personal archetypes and the life experiences these universal patterns bring into their lives.

Website: *www.myss.com*

BILL GUGGENHEIM

Bill is a pioneer in the field of After-Death Communication (ADC) experiences. He is considered to be the "father of ADC research" and has written and spoken on this subject for more than 25 years.

A native of New York City, Bill did not always embrace the beliefs he has now. During his first 35 years, he regarded himself as an agnostic, choosing to see life through the lens of "rational materialism". During this time, Bill was a stockbroker and a securities analyst on Wall Street and had no interest in spiritual matters. He believed "When you're dead, you're dead."

In 1974, Bill experienced a spiritual awakening that would shape the rest of his life. He began receiving messages from the "other side" that affirmed life after death—something he did not believe in. "I received messages from people who had already made their transition, many of whom I did not know personally" Bill says. "They asked me to share their messages with their family members and friends who were living. Frankly, I thought I was having a nervous breakdown." However, with the steady support of his former wife, Judy Guggenheim, Bill was able to navigate through this transformation, and came to see his experiences as a "spiritual breakthrough."

Bill immersed himself in spiritual teachings from a wide variety of sources, both Eastern and Western. He studied with different teachers such as Dr. Elizabeth Kubler-Ross and Rev. Anne Gehman to expand his concept of reality.

During the years that followed, Bill sought answers to life's oldest and most profound questions. He and his wife Judy founded The ADC Project to conduct the first in-depth research of After-Death Communications. During their seven years of research, they interviewed 2,000 people and collected more than 3,300 firsthand accounts from people who believed they had been contacted by a deceased family member or friend.

Their book *Hello From Heaven*—the first book published on the topic of After-Death Communication—was published in 1995. It has now been published in many languages.

Since *Hello From Heaven* was published, Bill has spoken at numerous conferences and appeared on a number of television and radio shows to spread the word about After-Death Communications. During that time, Bill made it his personal mission to help those who are grieving the loss of a loved one and validate ADC experiences as a "normal and natural part of life".

Bill states, "In my mind, receiving a message from a loved one who has died is as common as receiving a greeting card from someone who is living. It is my hope that this understanding will someday be embraced and shared by all of humanity."

Websites: *www.billguggenheim.com* and *www.after-death.com*

BERNIE SIEGEL, M.D.

Dr. Siegel, who prefers to be called Bernie, not Dr. Siegel, was born in Brooklyn, NY. He attended Colgate University and Cornell University Medical College. He holds membership in two scholastic honor societies, Phi Beta Kappa and Alpha Omega Alpha and graduated with honors. His surgical training took place at Yale New Haven Hospital, West Haven Veteran's Hospital and the Children's Hospital of Pittsburgh. He retired from practice as an assistant clinical professor of surgery at Yale of general and pediatric surgery in 1989 to speak to patients and their caregivers.

In 1978, he originated Exceptional Cancer Patients, a specific form of individual and group therapy utilizing patients' drawings, dreams, images and feelings. ECaP is based on "carefrontation," a safe, loving therapeutic confrontation, which facilitates personal lifestyle changes, personal empowerment, and healing of the individual's life. The physical, spiritual and psychological benefits that followed led to his desire to make everyone aware of his or her healing potential. He realized exceptional behavior is what we are all capable of.

His books include:

Love. Medicine & Miracles 1986, *Peace, Love & Healing* 1989, *How To Live Between Office Visits* 1993, *Prescriptions for Living 1998*, *Help Me To Heal* 2003, *365 Prescriptions For The* Soul, *Smudge Bunny* 2004, *101 Exercises For The Soul* 2005, *Love, Magic & Mud Pies* 2006, *Buddy's Candle* 2008, *Faith, Hope & Healing* 2009, *Words Swords, A Book of Miracles* 2011, *The Art of Healing* 2013.

Bernie, and his wife and coworker Bobbie, live in a suburb of New Haven, Connecticut. They have five children and eight grandchildren. Their home with its many children, pets and interests resembled a cross between a family art gallery, museum, zoo and automobile repair shop. It still resembles these things, although the children are trying to improve its appearance in order to avoid embarrassment.

He is currently working on other books with the goal of humanizing medical education and medical care as well as empowering patients and teaching survival behavior to enhance immune system competency. His prediction is that in the next decade the role of consciousness, spirituality, non-local healing, body memory and heart energy will all be explored as scientific subjects.

Bernie has touched many lives all over our planet. In 1978 he began talking about patient empowerment and the choice to live fully and die in peace. As a physician who has cared for and counseled innumerable people whose mortality has been threatened by an illness, Bernie embraces a philosophy of living and dying that stands at the forefront of the medical ethics and spiritual issues our society grapples with today. He continues to assist in the breaking of new ground in the field of healing and personally struggling to live the message of kindness and love.

Website: *www.BernieSiegelMD.com*

STAN GROF, M.D., PH.D.

Dr. Grof is a psychiatrist with more than fifty years of experience researching non-ordinary states of consciousness. He has been the principal investigator in a psychedelic research program at the Psychiatric Research Institute in Prague; Chief of Psychiatric Research at the Maryland Psychiatric Research Center; Assistant Professor of Psychiatry at the Johns Hopkins University in Baltimore; and Scholar-in-Residence at the Esalen Institute in Big Sur.

Currently, he is a Professor of Psychology at the California Institute of Integral Studies (CIIS) in San Francisco. He conducts professional training programs in Holotropic Breathwork and transpersonal psychology. Dr. Grof also presents lectures and seminars worldwide. He is one of the founders and chief theoreticians of transpersonal psychology and the founding president of the International Transpersonal Association (ITA).

In 2007, Grof was granted the prestigious Vision 97 Award from the Václav and Dagmar Havel Foundation in Prague. In 2010, he was given the Thomas R. Verny Award from the Association for Pre- and Perinatal Psychology and Health (APPPAH) for his pivotal contributions to this field.

Among his publications are over 150 articles in professional journals. His books include *LSD: Gateway to the Numinous; Beyond the Brain; LSD Psychotherapy; The Cosmic Game; Psychology of the Future; The Ultimate Journey; When the Impossible Happens; Healing Our Deepest Wounds.* The co-authored with Christina Grof: *The Stormy Search for the Self; Spiritual Emergency;* and *Holotropic Breathwork.*

Website: *www.stanislavgrof.com_*

KAREN WYATT, M.D.

Dr. Wyatt graduated from the University of New Mexico School of Medicine and completed Family Practice Residency and a Fellowship in Psychiatry at the University of Utah. She spent her 25-year medical career working with patients in challenging settings, such as hospices, nursing homes and indigent clinics.

Dr. Wyatt founded a free medical clinic in a homeless shelter, accompanied three medical mission teams to Honduras, and led a non-profit clinic for the uninsured in its growth from a 4-hour per week all-volunteer operation to a full-time, full-service medical center. She has twice testified at Senate briefings on the cutting edge model of integrated medical care, combining physical and behavioral health, which she helped create and implement in her clinic for the uninsured.

Dr. Wyatt is a founding member of the Integral Health and Medicine Center where she has taught about the application of Integral Theory to medical care, particularly at the end of life. Motivated by her compassionate heart, she has put her spiritual beliefs into action by being of service to others in need and developing Creative Healing, an initiative to integrate spirituality into traditional medical practice.

Inspired by her work as a hospice medical director Dr. Wyatt has written extensively about end-of-life care, including the book "What Really Matters: 7 Lessons for Living from the Stories of the Dying," which describes the spiritual lessons she learned from her hospice patients. She is also the author of "A Matter of Life & Death: Stories to Heal Loss & Grief." She lectures frequently to medical and lay audiences about spirituality and the end-of-life.

Dr. Wyatt also hosts an online interview series entitled End-of-Life University (www.eoluniversity.com), which features interviews and conversations about all aspects of the end-of-life. She has won numerous awards for her volunteer service including the Spirit of the American Woman Award and being named one of Utah's 100 Notable Women. She has been featured in USA Today, Publisher's Weekly, Huffington Post, Shift Magazine, Light of Consciousness Journal, the Denver Post and numerous medical journals.

Dr. Wyatt teaches that in order to live life fully we must overcome our fear of death and embrace the difficulties that life brings us. She is an inspired teacher who truly embodies the message she brings to the world. She is married with two children and lives in Colorado.

Website: *www.karenwyattmd.com*

Facebook at *fb.com/karenwyattmd*

Twitter *@spiritualmd*

MARK ANTHONY, J.D.

Mark Anthony the Psychic Lawyer® is a world-renowned fourth generation psychic medium who communicates with spirits. He graduated with honors from Mercer University Law School which included the study of law at Oxford University in England. Mark is licensed to practice law in Florida, Washington D.C. and before the United States Supreme Court. In England, he studied mediumship at the prestigious Arthur Findlay College for the Advancement of Psychic Science.

Mr. Anthony is featured regularly as a psychic medium, paranormal expert, and legal analyst in high profile murder cases on ABC, CBS, NBC, and FOX Television. He also has been interviewed on major talk radio shows such as Coast to Coast AM, Darkness Radio, and Sirius XM. He is a featured speaker about the afterlife at conventions, expos and spiritual organizations such as the Edgar Cayce Association for Research and Enlightenment and universities including Harvard, Brown and Yale.

Mark's best-selling and award nominated book *Never Letting Go* is the definitive guide to healing grief with help from the Other Side. His groundbreaking book *Evidence of Eternity* is a major spiritual bestseller that explains spirit communication with science, theoretical physics, physiology and evidence.

Website: *www.EvidenceOfEternity.com*

To view videos about *Evidence of Eternity* visit:
http://youtu.be/A9XK0Eb1VZc

RAYMOND MOODY, M.D., PH.D.

Dr. Moody is a best-selling author of twelve books including *Life After Life*—which has sold over 13 million copies world wide—and *Reunions*. He has also written numerous articles for academic and professional literature. Dr. Moody continues to capture enormous public interest and generate controversy with his ground-breaking work on the near-death experience and what happens when we die.

He received the World Humanitarian Award in Denmark in 1988. He was also honored with a bronze medal in the Human Relations category at the New York Film Festival for the movie version of *Life After Life*. In 2015, Dr. Moody will receive the first-ever Afterlife Awareness Award in Norfolk, VA.

Dr. Moody is the leading authority on the 'near-death experience'—a phrase he coined in the late seventies. His research into this phenomenon began in the 1960's and the *New York Times* called him "the father of the near-death experience." His training includes:

- Ph.D. in philosophy from the University of Virginia, 1969

- M.A. in philosophy from the University of Virginia, 1967

- B.A. with Honors in philosophy from the University of Virginia, 1966

Dr. Moody has enlightened and entertained audiences all over the world for over three decades. He offers many different lecture/workshop presentations on the topics of:

- Near Death Experiences

- Death With DignityLife After Loss: Surviving Grief and Finding Hope

- Reunions: Visionary Encounters With Departed Loved Ones

- The Healing Power of Humor

- The Loss of Children

- Catastrophic Tragedies and Events Causing Collective Grief Response.

He trains hospice workers, clergy, psychologists, nurses, doctors, and other medical professionals on matters of grief recovery and dying. Dr Moody has appeared three times on Oprah, as well as on hundreds of other local and nationally syndicated programs such as MSNBC: Grief Recovery, NBC Today, ABC's Turning Point, Donahue, Sally Jessy Raphael Show, Geraldo, and The Joan Rivers Show.

He is a frequent presenter at conferences around the county. In addition, Dr. Moody works counsels and consults on an individual basis in person, by phone, or at the bedside of the dying.

Website: *www.lifeafterlife.com*

NEXT STEPS...

The guests and I offer powerfully transformative products and services to help you further awaken and live the greatest life you have envisioned. To learn more about theirs, visit the websites listed at the bottom of their Biography pages. Here's an overview of mine:

- *Soul Proof book* with foreword by Bernie Siegel and with exclusive contributions from Wayne Dyer, Raymond Moody, and others. Discusses nine categories of evidence—with special focus on documented clinical and scientific research—that collectively indicates we each are infinite beings of energy/consciousness.

- *Soul Proof movie:* a 93-minute film interviewing people who had personal experiences such as NDEs, ADCs, miracles, perinatal experiences, etc. Also videos of experts such as Moody, Bill Guggenheim, Michael Newton, and others.

- *Radiant Wellness book:* 7 keys to fine-tuning the body/mind so it's congruent, on the same wavelength, as your essence. That assists remembering that this earth-experience is a totally safe and magnificent adventure amidst eternity.

- *The Eleven Questions:* commonly asked questions about life, death and afterlife. Exclusive interviews by Dr. Pitstick with Raymond Moody, PhD, MD, Caroline Myss, MA, Anita Moorjani, Bernie Siegel, MD, Stan Grof, MD, PhD, Gary Schwartz, PhD, Bill Guggenheim, P.M.H. Atwater, Marilyn Schlitz, PhD, Karen Wyatt, MD, Mark Anthony, JD

- *Transformational CDs:* 2 hour CDs to help you release energetic blocks, old wounds, limiting teachings, and really awaken to the great news that sets you free. (The first three are done under hypnosis/deep relaxation.)

    - **Ask Your Soul:** a chance to address one's inner wisdom and receive feedback about your toughest questions and quandaries

    - *Healing Your Past:* releasing old wounds and stuck energy from earlier in this life and perhaps other times/places

    - *Your life review:* if you died today, what would your life review be like? Find out, then identify areas for improvement so it's a work of art when you really do pass on.

    - *Holistic Breathwork:* 45 minutes of deep breathing with a background of coaching and outrageous music to facilitate releasing any blocks that keep you from realizing who you are, why you're here, and Who walks beside you always.

Soul Proof Productions™
www.soulproof.com mark@soulproof.com 740-701-9793

ABOUT THE AUTHOR

Mark Pitstick, M.A., D.C., has over forty years' experience and training in hospitals, pastoral counseling settings, mental health centers and private practice. His training includes a premedical degree, graduate theology/pastoral counseling studies, masters in clinical psychology, and doctorate in chiropractic health care.

After working in hospitals with many suffering and dying adults and children, Mark was motivated to find sensible, evidence-based answers to the questions answered in this book.

His books, movie, CDs, online classes, and experiential workshops address all of these questions and help you survive and thrive throughout life's biggest changes and challenges. Further, his work helps you discover how to enjoy the greatest life you have envisioned—no matter what your current circumstances.

He was certified in *Past Life Regression* therapy by Brian Weiss, M.D., and the *After-Death Contact* technique by Raymond Moody, M.D. He has also provided suicide prevention counseling and education to many.

Dr. Pitstick wrote *Soul Proof: Compelling Evidence You Are an Infinite Energetic/ Spiritual Being.* He is also the author of *Radiant Wellness: A Holistic Guide for Optimal Body, Mind & Spirit.* His books have been endorsed by Drs. Wayne Dyer, Elisabeth Kubler-Ross, Deepak Chopra, Bernie Siegel, Ken Ring, and others.

Mark was the executive producer for the *Soul Proof* documentary film, a 93-minute movie featuring interviews with people who had near-death experiences, after-death contacts, miracles, paranormal encounters, and experts on these topics.

He also created three transformational CDs that assist spiritual awareness and optimal wellness with hypnosis/deep relaxation: *Ask Your Soul, Healing Your Past, and Your Life Review.* Mark also facilitates group *transformational breathwork.*

A frequent radio and TV guest, Pitstick hosted *Soul-utions,* a nationally syndicated radio show about soul issues and practical spirituality. He also hosted the *Ask the Soul Doctors* radio show and interviewed top consciousness experts.

Dr. Pitstick teaches online classes and nationwide workshops on spiritual awareness and optimal wellness. He has been a contributor to many magazines and currently writes a Q & A for Helping Parents Heal, a bereaved parents group, and articles for *www.eternea.org.*

Made in the USA
Monee, IL
10 June 2026

53029984R00101